BILLY HALL

---◆---

SAM AND THE SHERIFF

Complete and Unabridged

LINFORD
Leicester

First published in Great Britain in 2014 by
Robert Hale Limited
London

First Linford Edition
published 2016
by arrangement with
Robert Hale Limited
London

A catalogue record for this book is available
from the British Library.

ISBN 978–1–4448–2896–2

Published by
F. A. Thorpe (Publishing)
Anstey, Leicestershire

Set by Words & Graphics Ltd.
Anstey, Leicestershire
Printed and bound in Great Britain by
T. J. International Ltd., Padstow, Cornwall

This book is printed on acid-free paper

1

The sharp crack of a rifle shattered the irenic peace of the mountainside. It carried on the high, dry air, echoing back from peaks and cliffs, repeating itself in ebbing volume from a dozen directions.

The tall man reined his horse off the trail into the edge of the timber. His head cocked to one side, he listened a long moment. He fixed in his mind the direction from which that first sound had come, before it was confused by all the echoes.

It might have been just some cowboy or sheepherder shooting a coyote. Or shooting at one. No, not shooting at one, he mused. If he were shooting at a coyote and missed, he'd have shot again. If it hadn't already gotten out of range, he'd have shot twice more.

It might have been a shot aimed at a

deer. Fresh venison was always welcome. The hand who rode in at the end of a day with a deer draped across his saddle was sure to bask in a brief moment of glory. His horse wouldn't be happy about carrying it home, but the rest of the hands would surely appreciate it.

The tall man's lips were drawn to a tight, straight line above his broad chin. It was obvious in his posture he didn't think it was either a coyote or a deer. Or anything else that benign.

'Too late already,' he muttered.

He glanced down at the dog standing a few feet away. He noted the canine's laid-back ears. His tail wasn't between his legs, but it was a long way from high and wagging. That dog had good instincts.

'Didn't like that, huh, Sam?'

The dog glanced up at him, then returned his gaze to the same direction he had been staring.

'Well, I guess we'd better go check it out,' he informed the shaggy animal.

Man and dog looked equally shaggy, for that matter. Hair trailed out beneath the man's hat as if its curly mass were too free-spirited to be held in check, even by a hat with that high a crown. The front of the crown was shaped by one large crease from the tip of the crown to the broad brim. Beneath that brim, pale blue eyes stared unblinkingly ahead.

He spoke to the dog again. 'Cover, Sam. Scout.'

The dog moved ahead, remaining in the edge of the timber instead of on the trail. Wherever brush or trees interfered with his progress, he skirted them on the timber side, never leaving the cover the forest provided. He moved like a silent shadow, almost instantly lost to the man's sight.

As if on a Sunday afternoon's pleasure ride, the man returned to the trail. He gave the horse his head, knowing the animal would maintain the distance between himself and the dog.

They were a seasoned trio. Sam, Ned

and Justus had covered a good many miles together. Ned had never been sure whether he had trained the horse and dog that well, or they had trained him. No matter. They were a team. They were a team to be reckoned with.

The star that caught the occasional rays of sunlight filtering through the trees was simply a part of him. Emblazoned on it was one word. 'Sheriff'.

He rode on nearly a mile. He rounded a curve in the trail he followed to find his dog standing in the middle of the trail, facing him. The dog's head was down close to the ground. His ears were forward. His tail touched the ground. Ned started to rein in his mount, then realized the horse had stopped without being told.

As soon as he stopped, the dog disappeared again.

Ned took a deep breath and moved his horse into the edge of the trees again. He lifted the strap from the hammer of the Colt forty-five on his

4

hip. He lifted the gun slightly, then let it drop back into its socket, confident nothing would hinder his drawing it if he needed to do so. He didn't expect to need it.

Twenty minutes later the dog appeared in the trail again. This time his head was up, ears perked forward, tail held high. As soon as Ned spotted him he turned and trotted away, following the trail. Once again without being told to do so the horse followed, lifting his gait to a swift trot to match the dog's pace.

Minutes later he found what he expected. A man lay face up in the middle of the trail. A round hole stared malevolently upward from his chest. A pool of already drying blood stained the ground on the downhill side of his torso. His eyes stared sightlessly, not even bothered by the fly that crawled across the right pupil.

Ned stepped to the ground. He didn't worry about the gunman still being in the area. Sam would have found where he had been when he fired the shot, and whether he was long gone. Having that dog saved him a full hour of circling and scouting, to ensure he wouldn't be the next target.

He knelt beside the dead man and went through his pockets. He found a pocket knife, though the man wore a large knife on his belt. He wore no pistol. His rifle would have been in the saddle scabbard.

A brick of Red Man Chewing Tobacco was in one back pocket. Other than a few coins, he carried little else. There was nothing to identify him, or who he worked for. It wasn't necessary anyway. 'Never even saw it comin', did you Cletus?' he addressed the dead man. 'Lars ain't gonna be a happy camper.'

'Did you find his horse?' he asked, again as if speaking to the dead man.

Sam sat down and stared at him. He lowered his head once, as if wishing he had the ability to speak, then lay down. It didn't matter. His master knew from his actions what the answer was.

Ned glanced up at the sky. 'Well, Cletus, that means whoever shot you took your horse,' he mused. 'I sure ain't gonna haul you on my horse and walk all the way to the Palisades to let Lars know what happened.'

He grasped the dead man beneath the arms and dragged him with surprising ease off the trail and to a dish-shaped declivity in the ground. He straightened him, folding his arms across his chest. Then he carried rocks, some weighing over a hundred pounds, until he had built a cairn over the corpse.

Standing there by himself, he didn't appear to be all that big a man. True, his shoulders were broad and rounded with bulging muscles. His waist was slender, and the muscles on his thighs rippled through his trousers as he lifted the heavier of the rocks. It was when he stood amongst other men that he stood out, nearly a foot taller than many of them, and probably sixty pounds heavier than most. None of it was fat.

With his shirtsleeve he wiped the sweat from his face. 'Well, that'll keep the varmints away from 'im, at least,' he said.

Mounting his horse, he rode to a high point a quarter-mile to his left. From there he could look across the broad mountain valley. Spread out before him, the nearest of them half a mile away, roughly 900 sheep grazed placidly. He spotted two dogs sitting on the far side of the sheep, keeping vigil. 'Chances are the dogs'll take 'em to water about sundown, without bein' told to,' he muttered. 'Either that or just stay with 'em and keep 'em bunched. They ain't likely to leave 'em till they're told to. I'll have to let Lars worry about that end o' things. That's about all I can do.'

There would be a lot more to do in the days to come, though. A sinking feeling tied his gut in a tight knot. This was only the beginning.

2

'Track 'im, Sam.'

Ned spoke the words in a conversational tone, as if talking across a table to a friend. The dog responded instantly. Not even appearing to search for a trail, he trotted off.

The sheriff nudged his horse gently with his boot heels. 'Stay with him, Justus,' he ordered the equine member of his private team. He really didn't need to say that either. The horse had already started to follow the canine guide. The whole scene appeared as if it had been scripted, or followed enough times for both dog and horse to know the drill.

Justus didn't break into a trot. He was a good walker. He could walk as fast as most horses could trot, and he could do so for several days on end when the need arose. He didn't look that exceptional. True, muscles rippled beneath the hide wherever you looked at him, but he wasn't that big a horse. At just over fifteen hands, it wasn't his size or strength that set him apart.

Once, in a bunkhouse conversation, a hand on one of the ranches he visited asked, 'What color o' horse do you ride, Sheriff?'

Those who knew the sheriff grinned, instantly confusing the questioner. Ned had hesitated for a long moment, then said, 'Well, that's sorta hard to say.'

'Hard to say what color he is?'

'Well, yeah. I guess he's sorrel. And black. And white. And buckskin. And dappled gray. Oh, yeah, I guess he's roan too, sorta, here and there.'

The fact was, Justus was all of those things. Mostly it might be said he was a pinto. They'd have called him a grulla in the southwest. Here in Wyoming Territory he was just a paint, or a pinto, but that designation didn't begin to do him justice. Maybe that's why Ned named him 'Justus'. Nothing else would quite do him justice.

The animal's background would probably be considered white. It was the patches of color that were distinctive. No two patches of darker color on the animal were the same. His face was mostly sorrel, with a white blaze down the center. The neck was black on one side, but almost palomino yellow on the other side. Behind an irregular strip of white at the withers, one side of his lower body was dappled gray, but the other side was roan. His mane was brown, as were both of his lower hind legs. The tail, however, instead of matching the mane, was white. In spite of his almost perfect form and contours, the crazy-quilt hodge-podge of colors made him appear strange to the point of grotesque.

But he was easily the smartest horse Ned had ever ridden. And the most fiercely loyal. No other man who tried to ride him had ever been able to stay in the saddle more than a few seconds. If they tried, the horse came unglued, and bucked in ways no cowboy had ever experienced.

Ned, on the other hand, could call him anywhere, any time. If Justus could hear him at all, he'd come at a gallop. Ned could hop on and ride him anywhere without saddle or bridle, guiding him only with a word or a shift of his body. Man, horse and dog seemed to be linked to the same brain at times in ways that were uncanny. The Shoshoni called the trio 'Bahai Mukua'. As nearly as Ned could translate, it meant three spirits bound together. Mostly they shortened it, and just called Ned 'Bahaitee', which simply meant 'Three'.

The horse followed the dog, who followed the scent through stands of timber, across slopes of gray shale, across a broad valley, then up across a high ridge. At the top of the ridge Ned pulled gently on the reins. As the horse stopped he whistled one short, soft note.

He sat in the saddle, chewing on his

lip for a long moment. Sam emerged from a stand of timber and sat on the ground, watching his master, waiting to be told what to do.

Ned took a deep breath. Whether thinking aloud or conversing with one or both animals, he said, 'Now what do we do? We're right at the edge o' the reservation. I ain't got no jurisdiction past this ridge.'

Neither animal offered an answer to his dilemma.

Ned glanced up at the sun, estimating the amount of daylight. 'He'll be pullin' up to find a camp site purty quick,' he guessed, 'unless he wants to fix his supper in the dark.'

He scratched the back of his neck thoughtfully. 'Crow Crick oughta be just down below a ways. Ten to one he'll camp along it. Well, we'd just as well see if we can catch up with him afore dark.'

He lifted the reins. As if reading his mind Sam wheeled and led the way again. Justus followed, keeping the same distance behind the dog as he had maintained from the start.

It was less than half an hour later when the dog stopped. He turned and sat down directly ahead of the horse and rider.

Wordlessly Ned slid from the saddle, lifting his thirty-thirty Winchester from the saddle scabbard as he did so. He dropped the reins, knowing Justus would stand silently until he returned, or until he called him.

Moving like a pair of shadows through the timber, man and dog crept silently forward. Ned caught a whiff of smoke for one instant before it was borne away by the light breeze. He stopped just inside the edge of the timber and surveyed the scene ahead of him.

Twenty yards from the edge of Crow Creek, a man bent over a small, smokeless fire. Beyond him two saddles lay upside down on the ground. A bedroll lay between the saddles and the fire, but was not yet unrolled. Beyond it all a pair of horses tore hungrily at the lush grass. With approval, Ned noted they were both picketed where they could drink at will from the creek.

At least he treats the horses better'n he does folks, he thought.

Lifting his rifle to his shoulder he yelled, 'Throw up your hands!'

At the first syllable the man flung himself to the side and rolled. He came to his feet facing Ned, his forty five already in his hand. It spat fire in Ned's direction at almost the same instant as Ned's rifle barked. Branches snapped above Ned's head as the man's shot went high and wide of its mark. That may have been because the leaden projectile from Ned's rifle slammed into him a scant instant before he pulled the trigger.

The impact of the bullet drove him back and down, slamming him against the ground. Both arms flopped outward. The pistol lay on top of his right hand, no longer gripped by fingers separated from the will of the man to whom they were attached. In the space of less than two seconds he had gone from a man anticipating a hot supper to a corpse.

Ned watched for a moment to make sure the man wasn't going to move. He already knew he wouldn't. A thirty-thirty slug from that close range would have exploded the man's heart on impact. He didn't even consider that he might have missed the focus of his aim.

With another glance around Ned walked to the man and kicked the gun away from the lifeless hand. 'Just as well you didn't throw up your hands like I told you,' he muttered. 'With Cletus's horse an' saddle, followed here by Sam, you'd have stretched a rope the day after I got you back to Buckroot.'

He added with a grimace, 'I mean Lander. Dang it! I wish they'd make up their mind what they call that town.'

He whistled once, sharply. Not waiting for Justus to emerge from the timber, he laid down his rifle and began pulling handfuls of green grass. He squatted beside the dead man's fire and began to toss green grass on to it, a little at a time. Instantly a slender spire of white smoke ascended.

At almost the same time, the coffee pot at the fire's edge began to boil over. Whipping off his neckerchief and using it as a pot holder, he grabbed the coffee pot and moved it away from the heat. He lifted the lid and tossed a dash of cold water from the canteen laying close by into the boiling liquid.

'No sense wastin' a good pot of Arbuckle,' he muttered. 'I'd just as soon use my own cup, though.'

As if in answer, Justus chose that moment to emerge from the timber. He walked with his head off to the side to avoid stepping on the reins, and walked directly to Ned. Swiftly the sheriff stripped saddle and bridle off. 'Stay close,' he ordered the animal. He made no effort to tether the gelding, knowing he wouldn't stray out of hearing of him, nor very far from the other horses that were tethered.

He rolled out his bedroll, fetched a

tin cup from it, and poured himself a cup of coffee. He sipped the dark liquid as he continued to toss grass on to the fire often enough to keep the spire of smoke consistent.

When he had finished the cup of coffee he walked over to Crow Creek. He eyed the rushing mountain stream carefully for a moment. He walked a circle to a spot he had picked, and approached the stream carefully. As he neared it, he rolled up the sleeves of his shirt and the long underwear beneath it. He crawled to the water's edge. Moving slowly he slid his hand and arm into the water, moving his hand carefully back under the creek bank, where the current had undercut the ground. Lifting his hand up slowly from the bottom of the creek, he felt the underbelly of a fish. As his hand contacted it, he clamped down hard on it and jerked it out of the water, flinging it away from the edge of the creek.

He stood and walked to it, then swiftly eviscerated it with the knife that hung from his belt. Then he dropped it on the ground, walked about twenty paces upstream and repeated the action. He eyed the two large cut-throat trout with approval.

'How's that for fishin', Sam?' he asked the dog, which studied his every move.

In response, or perhaps in anticipation, Sam licked his lips and wagged his tail.

After returning to the camp fire Ned used a boot to scrape away some of the ashes of the fire. He laid the two trout on the remaining ashes, glowing red. Then with his boot he kicked burning embers over the top of them, burying them in the hot coals.

He chewed on his bottom lip thoughtfully for a moment, glancing around the cleared area. 'I 'spect I oughta do a couple more,' he decided.

Fifteen minutes later he had two more fish roasting in the coals on the other side of the fire. 'If you don't want fish for supper you could go catch a rabbit,' he told the dog.

He already knew what the dog's response would be. He glanced at the timber, then scooted closer to the fire, eyeing the spot where the trout roasted. Strange as it seemed, there were few things Sam liked as well as fish. One of those Ned had caught was plenty for himself. The other one was for Sam. As another facet of the dog's odd unpredictability, he preferred them cooked, with the bones removed.

An hour later the camp site was cloaked in darkness. Ned sat thirty yards back from the fire he had allowed to die down to barely glowing embers. The two fish from one side of the fire had been eaten. After they were roasted, it was a simple matter to peel away the skin and scales from one side, then lift the meat from that side of the fish carefully. It lifted away from the bones, leaving the fish's skeleton intact and the meat boneless. It made a fine meal.

Sam had scarfed down the one Ned

deboned for him in two bites.

The darkness deepened. Somewhere an owl called softly. The air chilled rapidly, prompting Ned to throw a blanket around his shoulders as he sat cross-legged on the ground. Somewhere down the creek he heard a bear grousing its way along the edge of the creek. Otherwise there was no sound.

Suddenly Sam growled once, softly. In the same instant he slunk away, disappearing in the dark. Ned nodded, listening intently. A few minutes later he said aloud, 'You fellas had just as well come on in. I cooked you a couple o' trout. They oughta still be warm under the fire there.'

There was no response for a long moment. Then the darkness moved slightly. Ned sensed, rather than saw, two shapes take form and move toward him in the gloom.

Wordlessly a pair of men moved to the fire. Using sticks, they stirred the ashes and found the fish Ned had left beneath the coals. They followed the same procedure he had followed, except they ate the heads that remained on them, along with the rest of the fish.

When they had finished, one of them said, 'Bahaitee.'

The moon had risen over the top of the Absaroka Mountains as they ate the fish. The soft moonlight was more than adequate for Ned, his eyes well accustomed to the darkness, to recognize the two Shoshone Indians.

'Deide-Haih,' he greeted one Shoshoni in his own tongue. He knew he preferred that to the translation — 'Little Crow' — just because it was his language. To the other he nodded and said, 'Baika-Dugaani — Kills At Night', being careful to greet the older of the pair first.

Knowing his command of their language was limited, Little Crow spoke in English from that point.

'You kill a man.'

Ned nodded silently.

'You are on our reservation. Shoshone land.'

Ned nodded again. 'He shot a man over on the other side of the ridge, outside of the reservation. I tracked him here. He shot at me.'

'He is known to you?'

'No. I have not seen him before.'

'Who did he kill?'

'A man by the name of Cletus Woodman. He herded the sheep of Lars Ingevold.'

'You knew this man who was killed?'

'I knew him.'

'He was your friend?'

'I just knew who he was.'

'Then why did you need to enter our reservation to avenge his death?'

'It is my duty. It is what a sheriff must do, as you do as the reservation police. You also cross that line if you are chasing a Shoshoni who has broken your laws.'

Silence hung heavily for several minutes. Ned did nothing to disturb it. At last Little Crow said, 'Ingevold is a good white man. Not like others, who think the Shoshone have no rights. He came to us when he wished to have sheep eat grass on our reservation. We made a treaty with him. He pays for our grass with sheep for our people every year. Always he gives us good sheep, never the sick ones or those that are old and hard to eat. We have grown to like them. That is why the Arapaho who share our reservation call us 'Tuku-aduka', 'The Sheep Eaters'.'

'Sheep are good meat.'

Little Crow nodded. 'They feed our people well. No longer do we have the dying time at the end of long winters. It is good. It is good that you kill the man who is the enemy of our friend, Ingevold.'

'I think he may have wanted others to think it was one of the Shoshone who killed the sheepherder. I have an idea that's why he took Cletus's horse and rode straight over here to the reservation. If someone who wasn't too good a tracker followed the trail, he'd think it was one of you who did it.'

'Who would wish to do so?'

'I don't know. When I find out who this fella is, I might have a better idea. There's some folks that don't want us round eyes bein' friends with you, though.'

Little Crow nodded his head knowingly. 'Some would cause us to go again on the warpath, so they can drive us from the land they have agreed is ours.'

'That might be it. I have been hearing rumors that some want war. I'll find out. I did want you to know who followed him here and killed him.'

'It is good that you sent the smoke, that we would know who came.'

'I do not wish to offend my friends, the Shoshone.'

Little Crow changed the subject abruptly. 'You do not tether your horse.'

Ned smiled, not at all surprised that they had noted that fact, even in the darkness.

'I do not need to. He will stay with me. He will come when I wish him to do so.'

'The dog that is bound to you is with you also.'

'He is here.'

'It is truly said that you are 'Bahaitee'. It is good you are friend of the Shoshone.'

'The Shoshone are a good people. I am proud to be a friend of the Shoshone.'

'We sleep now,' Little Crow said, with no further formalities.

He and Kills At Night moved to the edge of the timber, rolled in their blankets, and went to sleep at once. 'Must've picketed their own horses afore they made their presence known,' Ned muttered.

He moved to his own bedroll, shucked his boots and slid into blankets. He barely noticed when Sam slid like a silent shadow from the timber and curled up against him. He slept soundly, confident the dog would alert him of any danger.

3

He heard the slight, furtive, scuffing sounds in the hour before dawn. Sam lay beside him, head up, alert, but sounding no warning. Ned took a cue from the canine and played possum.

From the sounds he knew the two Shoshoni were stripping the things they wanted from the dead man, and readying their horses. They rode quietly out of camp within a few minutes.

Ned crawled from his blankets. He checked his boots for unwanted visitors and slipped his feet into them. He stretched the ache out of his joints and muscles. His mind was churning all the while.

He would find out when it got a little lighter whether the Indians had left the dead man's horse, or had considered that their rightful property too. He knew they would do so with any of the man's belongings they chose to take. He had invaded the reservation. He had been killed for his crimes. Whatever he bore with him or wore upon him was the rightful property of the Shoshone now.

He knew, too, that they would intend that the body be left where it was. It too belonged to the land of the Shoshone. It would feed the bears or the coyotes, the magpies, the wart-necked turkey buzzards, and numerous smaller scavengers. The bones would be gnawed by animals large and small for their minerals. It bothered Ned to leave the body of even a cold-blooded killer to that fate, but he knew better than to offend the customs of those upon whose tolerance his own fate rested, any time he needed to venture on to the reservation.

He built a small fire and used the dead man's coffee pot again to make his morning coffee. He did use his own coffee. He contented himself with a couple dried, brick-hard biscuits softened by dunking them in the coffee, and a piece of jerky.

As the sun rose behind the rim of the mountains soft light flooded the valley. He noted with surprise that the Indians had taken neither the dead man's horse nor the one that had belonged to Cletus. The saddles, of course, they ignored. They had taken the rifle, the lariat, and most likely whatever the saddle-bags held from one of the saddles. The one belonging to the slain sheepherder they left untouched.

'I wonder how they figured out which one belonged to who,' he asked of nobody in particular.

Within the hour he had saddled his own horse and the other two as well. He tied the reins of each bridle together and looped them over their respective saddle horns. Then he rigged a lariat from his own horse to the chinstrap of each of the other two bridles, allowing adequate slack for them to trail along single file behind him.

By the time the full orb of the sun had risen above the mountains he was retracing the path of the previous day's travel. It was high noon by the time he rode into the yard of The Palisades, the ranch of Lars Ingevold.

It was easy to see where Lars had gotten the name for the spread. Immediately behind the site of the ranch yard was a tall cliff rising in a series of giant upthrusts that bore an eerie resemblance to a gigantic stockade wall. It sheltered the ranch from the worst of winter storms. It also extended for as far as he could see to the south and east, providing a large, sheltered meadow that would be ideal for lambing time.

The procession of a rider leading two riderless horses drew instant attention.

'Goot midday, Sheriff. Get down and come in,' Lars greeted in his heavy accent.

Then he added, 'I tank dat ist Cletus's horse. Vat has happened to my herder?'

Ned stepped out of the saddle and gripped the extended hand of the rancher. 'Sorry to have to bring it home like this,' he said.

'Vat has happened to my herder?' Lars repeated.

'A fella shot 'im from ambush, is about all I can tell you. I don't think he ever saw it comin'. I buried him as best I could, in that narrow meadow that runs along the red cliff.'

'Shirt-Sleeve Canyon,' Lars identified.

'Who shot Cletus?' queried a second man who had walked across the yard to join them.

'I didn't recognize him.'

'Did you get 'im?'

Ned nodded, gesturing toward the second horse. 'I trailed him over on to the reservation. I tried to arrest him, but he went for his gun.'

'You rode on to the reservation und shot him der?' The concern in Lars's voice was equally telegraphed by his expression.

'Yeah,' Ned conceded. 'But I sent up a smoke signal to fetch the reservation police. Little Crow and Kills At Night came to check things out. I told 'em what the deal was, and they seemed OK with it. They took his guns and whatever they thought oughta belong to them.'

Lars's eyes probed the sheriff's deeply for a long moment. Then he said, 'So it vill not be the problem for my sheep vith the Indians?'

'No,' Ned assured him. 'They're plumb happy with the sheep you give 'em for runnin' 'em on their land.'

'Someone from the I Bar W, sure's anything,' the other man opined, a hard edge on his voice.

'Why do you say that?' Ned demanded.

'Who else would shoot a sheepherder in cold blood? We been squabblin' with them over grazin' rights for the last three or four years.'

'Who said it was in cold blood?' Ned demanded. 'I just said he got shot. What makes you think they wasn't arguin' over a woman or somethin'?'

The man opened his mouth twice as if to say something.

When the silence got awkward, Lars

addressed his foreman, 'Ray, Rodriguez ist back from helping to move der red band to high country, I tank?'

'Yeah. He got back in last night.'

'Take him up dere to herd Cletus's band. Stay vith him a day or two to be sure he ist able to handle Cletus's dogs.'

'That shouldn't be a problem,' Ray acknowledged. 'He's pretty good with the sheep and the dogs both.'

He walked over to the horses Ned was leading and untied the rope from the one that had been Cletus's mount. He led the horse away without saying anything more, or acknowledging Ned's presence again.

'What's eatin' Ray?' the sheriff asked the sheepman.

Lars looked uncomfortable. 'It is der things that Milosevitch hast put into his head, I suppose,' he offered. 'He tells all of der herders dat you are alvays on der cattlemen's side in eferyting.'

'Leo's been around clear out here?'

'Oh, yah. Yah, he comes here sometimes, and he goes vith der campjack sometimes to move a herder, so he can tell eferyvun how much better the sheriff he vould be dan you are. He can talk goot enough to convince folks dat der sun vill not come up tomorrow unless he tells it to do so.'

'I figgered he'd stop campaignin' once the election was over.'

'Oh, no, I don't tank he vill stop. He vill be der to run against you two years from now again. He tinks maybe he can spend all der time between now and then to make you look as bad as he can, so den maybe folks vill vote for him next time.'

'I'd think he'd have to do somethin' to make a livin', sometime.'

'Dat is vun of der tings I tink, sometimes. I don't know vat he does to make money.'

He changed the subject abruptly. 'Vat vill you do vith der man's horse you have shot?'

Ned almost said, 'I didn't shoot the horse,' but he stopped himself. Instead he said, 'I'll take 'im on into town.

Somebody might recognize the horse or know his brand. I really want to know who the guy was and why he shot your herder. Anyway, I guess, by law it belongs to the county now.'

Lars nodded. 'I vould like to know who it is dat done dat, too. If you had not followed him, I vould have tought maybe der Indians, maybe der cattlemen. Somevun ist trying to start a range var, I tank.'

'Sure looks that way. But who? And why?'

'I guess dat ist your job to find out. But you vill not find out standing here. Put your horses up in der barn and come on into der house. The missus vill have supper ready after a vile, and ve can visit vile ve vait.'

Supper was a special treat. Ingred Ingevold was an excellent cook. But it was the bubbly presence of their three daughters that made the meal delightful. They were stereotypical Scandinavian blondes, their hair so light it was almost white, their eyes deep sparkling blue, each a stair-step shorter image of the next older. Heidi, the middle daughter, constantly teased and baited Hildagarde, the elder, especially whenever Leo Milosevitch was mentioned.

'Hilda's in love with him,' Heidi announced as soon as his name was mentioned.

'I am not!' Hilda insisted.

'Are so! I seen how you hang around him, batting your eyes, giggling at everything he says.'

'I do not!'

'You blush every time he looks at you.'

Helga intervened, obviously bothered that her sisters bickered in the presence of an outsider. 'Heidi, you're embarrassing her. That's not polite when we have company.'

'Oh, what do you know about it?' Heidi demanded. 'You're only thirteen. You don't know anything.'

'I know when you're being rude,' Helga insisted.

'You don't think it's rude for Hilda to

be so syrupy sweet when that man butters her up about how pretty she is, and how smart she is, and how much he enjoys her intelligent conversation, and how well she rides, and — '

'Heidi! That's enough!' Ingred finally intervened. 'We do have company.'

By the time supper was over Ned had learned he didn't want to have to raise any daughters. Of course, if he and Nellie ended up marrying, their children wouldn't be at all like Ingevold's. Or so he told himself.

He also learned, during the course of the meal, that someone had randomly shot sheep in three of Lars' bands. One of the sheep wagons had been set afire while the herder was out with the sheep. Two of his dogs had been poisoned with strychnine. It was more than clear that someone was either trying to get rid of the sheepman, or to goad him into retaliating against whomever he suspected of the attacks against him.

The problem was, he had not the

least idea who might be behind it, or why. He clearly wasn't buying into the idea that the I Bar W was behind it. Neither did Ned, but knew he'd better find out, if he didn't want the lid blowing off the whole county.

4

'Well, there's Neversweat,' Sheriff Ned Garman said aloud, using the older, though unofficial name of the town that lay before him.

His horse pranced sideways with uncustomary impatience. It had been a long trail, and he was more than ready for rest and grain. 'Yeah, yeah, I know,' Ned offered, but he made no move to nudge the animal forward.

From the low hill where he had stopped, he could see the town of Dubois strung out along the Wind River. Off to his right the Absaroka Mountains, called 'The Absaracks' by the locals, soared more than 12,000 feet. The crests of their snowcapped peaks looked much closer than their thirty five miles or so from town. Far off, to his left, the craggier peaks of the Teton Range boasted even greater elevation, also capped with snow throughout the summer.

After surveying the town a long while he allowed the horse to proceed. He immediately broke into a swift trot. Ned grinned.

'Nothin' gives you a fit of energy quicker'n thinkin' you're gonna get to hole up in a barn and rest a while, does it?' he chided the animal, as if he could understand everything he said.

The dog that trailed along beside was noticeably less enthusiastic about coming to a town. To him every town had a plethora of mixed excitements and dangers. There were always other dogs there. Some were curious and friendly. Some were wary and territorial. Some were just plain mean, always seeking a weaker dog to attack. And then, some were female. Along every street were hundreds of strange scents to notice and sort out. Away from town, he could warn his master of impending danger. In town he didn't know who or what was dangerous, or how to make the determination.

Ah, but there were also cats! Not the wild, keep-their-distance, never-give-a-dog-a-chance barn cats that most ranches kept to minimize rodents and vermin around the buildings. Town cats. Cats that thought they should be liked and sheltered and petted and such. They were always fun. He had learned his master was not pleased if he chanced to kill or injure one. Not understanding politics, he didn't know why. But he could surely make them think they were about to die when he put them to flight. He didn't really hate cats. It's just that they were . . . well . . . cats.

Still a good quarter-mile short of town Ned hauled his horse to a stop in front of a long building made of logs, topped by a sod roof. A sign in front identified it as Welty's General Store. He draped the reins across the hitch rail without tying them. The dead killer's horse remained tethered to the saddle horn by the lariat lead rope.

'Stay here, Sam,' he ordered.

41

Obediently the dog sat down right at the end of the hitch rail, only his laid-back ears telegraphing his displeasure.

Ned stepped in the front door of the store and stopped, letting his eyes adjust to the dim interior.

Two pot-bellied stoves stood equally spaced along the interior, mid-way between front and rear. At one end a counter was crowded with small goods for sale, including four large jars of penny candy. Only the center was bare, to allow a place for folks to pay for what they purchased.

The rest of the store was filled floor to ceiling with stacks of dry goods, shelves of merchandise, barrels of pickles, crackers and such. In every convenient corner there was a stack of miscellaneous tools and implements leaning against the wall. Around each of the stoves a number of chairs were scattered. Not much went on in town that wasn't known and discussed at length around those two stoves. Several of the men sitting there nodded a silent greeting to Ned.

Frank Welty looked up from behind the counter as Ned walked in. 'Well, howdy, Sheriff,' he greeted. 'What brings you to Dubois?'

He pronounced it so the ending sounded like 'noise', instead of the French pronunciation.

With a straight face Ned said, 'I thought it was 'Doobwaaa',' drawing the end out with extra emphasis.

Welty spat on the floor of his own store. 'You'll never hear anyone around here say it like some high-falutin foreigner! If it wasn't for them dad-blamed politicians it'd still be 'Neversweat', like it was meant to be.'

'Doobwaa does sound a lot more dignified,' Ned argued. 'Downright continental, in fact.'

'Did you come in here to pick a fight or you gonna buy somethin'?'

'You best not get Frank too riled up, Sheriff,' a man piped up from beside the nearer of the two stoves. 'He built this here store outside o' town just 'cause they went an' changed the name of it.'

'What're you gonna do if someone builds another store half a mile up the road so they're inside the town?' Ned needled the merchant.

'Let 'em,' Frank spat out. 'Now you buyin', or just chinnin'?'

'Aw, I gotta rib somebody now an' then,' Ned defended.

'You better remember there'll be another 'lection comin' up afore you know it,' the storekeeper threatened with mock anger.

'Ask him if he voted for you last time,' a second voice from the stove suggested.

Welty snorted. 'I sure didn't vote for the slick-talkin' weasel that was runnin' against ya,' he declared. 'But since I did vote for you, you oughta at least buy somethin', hadn't ya?'

'Well, now, I don't know. Would that be tryin' to buy your vote?' Ned chided.

'It just might be. Give 'er a try. My

next vote just might just depend on how much you spend.'

'Somebody run an' tell the gov'nor!' the first speaker from the gossip circle yelled. 'There's vote-sellin' goin' on in Neversweat!'

'Dubois,' the second corrected. 'It's the governor that sent Neversweat floatin' off down the river.'

Tiring of the exchange, Ned's tone of voice changed. 'I need a couple boxes o' thirty-thirty shells, some Arbuckle and a pound or so of jerky.'

'Beef or elk?'

'You got elk?'

'Naw, not really. It's all beef. But if you want elk, I'll sell you some and call it elk. Beef's ten cents a pound. Elk's fifteen.'

'I sorta favor beef,' Ned decided. 'I got a horse I'd like you to have a look at, too.'

'Ain't tradin' horses. You gotta see Shorty at the livery barn for that.'

'I ain't sellin' 'im. I just wanta know if you know who he belongs to.'

Welty's eyes grew cautious. 'You find one runnin' loose?'

Silence filled the store clear up to the dried roots trailing below the sod roof. Every man by both stoves was leaning forward on his chair, lest he miss a word of what was said. 'I had to shoot the owner,' he said.

'How come?'

'He bushwhacked one of Lars' herders. I trailed 'im over on to the reservation. I yelled at him to throw up his hands, but he took a shot at me instead.'

'You didn't know him?'

'You followed him on to the reservation?' one of the loungers quizzed.

'No, I didn't know him. And yeah, I followed him on to the reservation.'

'That's gonna cause trouble,' another opined.

'No, it's OK. I cleared it with the reservation police.'

'They let you do that?' yet another demanded.

'They weren't real happy about it,

but they let it slide.'

'So what'd'ya want from me?' Frank asked, clearly irritated with the side-tracks to the discussion.

'I'd just like you to have a look at the horse. See if you recognize it.'

Frank shrugged and walked out from behind the counter. Ned followed, trailed by five men who had been lounging around the stoves. Ned silently cursed himself. He had never noticed the fifth man. He must have been sitting on the far side of the second stove. That kind of carelessness could cost him his life.

The group gathered in a silent half-circle, looking the horse in question up and down. Frank stroked his chin thoughtfully. 'Can't say as I recognize 'im.'

'Nevada Weston.'

All eyes turned to one of the idlers who had trailed outside with the rest. He was older than the others; his long hair, reaching his shoulders, was well streaked with gray. His large mustache was almost entirely white, the ends of it trailing below his jawline.

'You know the horse?' Ned pressed.

The old-timer nodded vigorously enough to wobble his mustache. 'Seen 'im around town three or four times. Belonged to a fella what called hisself Nevada Weston.'

'Do you know who he worked for?'

'Nobody, far as I know. Hardcase type. Drank a bit, but never got drunk. Gambled a bit, if there was a poker game goin'. Favored poker. Didn't never play monte. Said he wasn't dumb enough to buck them kinda odds. Mostly plumb tight-lipped.'

'It sounds like you're describin' a hired gun or an outlaw.'

The old fellow nodded again. 'He'd fit that picture all right enough.'

'Did he have any friends? Hang out with anyone in particular?'

'Nope. Pretty much a loner. Oh, he talked to that slick-talkin' fella what run against you for sheriff, but that there's just Milo. He'd strike up a conversation with a fence post and leave with the fence post braggin' to everyone about how good he drove staples into it, an' how proud it was to hold up that dad-gummed barbed wire, just so long as it was Milo's wire.'

As the group chuckled appreciatively Ned caught a fleeting glimpse of one of the group slipping away. He didn't notice any details, just a fleeting glimpse as the man ducked around the corner of the general store and disappeared.

'So whatcha gonna do with the horse an' saddle, Sheriff?'

'I'll give you thirty bucks for it,' another offered. 'Ten for the horse, twenty for the saddle and bridle.'

Ned shook his head. 'I got no right to sell it,' he refused. 'It belongs to the county.'

'What's the county gonna do with a horse an' saddle?'

'Sell it to help pay my salary.' Ned grinned. 'Of course, they'll spend fifty or sixty dollars to bring in the best horse trader the county commissioners know to sell it for 'em. They'll pay him twenty more for expenses while he's here to sell it. Then they'll tell you boys how much money they made for the county by sellin' this horse.'

One of the group turned and spat on the ground. He said, 'Yeah, an' that horse trader'll sell it for half what it's worth, then go around behind the barn an' have the guy that bought it sign it over to him, an' he'll ride outa town on it big as you please.'

'Well, it's nice to see you boys know how government works.' Ned grinned.

He went back inside and paid for the things he'd already selected. As he stepped back out he took extra time scanning every shadowed nook up and down the road. The hair on the back of his neck tingled as if stirred by some breeze that touched nothing else. He shifted the bag of merchandise to his left hand, dropping the right to brush the butt of his forty-five. Nothing seemed out of place.

He glanced down at Sam. The dog sat where he had been told to stay, watching his master with expressionless eyes. 'You're no help in town at all. Do you know that?' he muttered to the loyal animal.

Sam squirmed a little and tentatively wagged his tail, sensing his master's unease but knowing nothing about its reason.

Keeping his back toward the store behind him as much as possible, Ned stowed the things he had purchased in his saddle-bags. After another long look around he said, 'Well, let's go on into town and get these horses tended to.'

He swung into the saddle and turned his horse back on to the road. 'OK, Justus,' he said, 'you can head for that barn you been wantin' now.'

Justus walked, but he walked with an eager gait, as if knowing that rest from a long ride on the trail was half a mile up the road. They almost got there.

As he entered Dubois's main street, Ned's eyes scanned the array of horses, buggies and wagons tied up along the street. Most were crowded close to the two saloons. Metal clanged against metal as the blacksmith pounded a piece of red-hot iron on his anvil, the echoes bouncing back from the wooden façades of storefronts. Four young boys shouted excitedly as they chased each other in some sort of game, of which only they knew the rules. Three ladies, one holding a parasol against the glare of a hot sun shining through the thin air of the high altitude, chatted as they walked along the board sidewalk. Somewhere out of sight a hammer beat a steady pattern of four or five strikes, then a pause, then four or five strikes, pause, as a carpenter drove nails into something under construction.

All the sights and sounds of a peaceful and rapidly growing town failed to assuage the sense of peril that kept Ned's eyes constantly darting here and there. He caught a hint of movement in the shadow between two buildings. For reasons he wouldn't have understood if he had bothered to analyse them, it set off alarms in his mind. He leaped from the saddle, landing on his feet in the road with his gun drawn. Just as his feet hit the earth his hat flew from his head. The response from his forty five was instant. His bullet struck the corner of the building where the movement had caught his eye. It sent a shower of slivers outward.

Ned whirled, stepped around his horse, reached across his saddle and aimed his gun once again at that same spot, using the horse for cover, waiting for a follow-up shot from his attacker. None came.

'Don't think I hit 'im,' he complained. 'Unless I put a few slivers in 'im.'

Some part of his mind noted that the street had fallen deadly silent. Those on the sidewalks had scrambled for the safety of whatever building they were near. The three ladies who had been talking as they walked ducked inside the first door they saw. They found themselves inside the Wind River saloon. They clustered at the door, mortified to be there, but too frightened to leave.

'Check it out, Sam,' Ned ordered.

Sam sprinted to the far side of the street, then ran along the fronts of buildings until he arrived at the opening between buildings from which the shot had come. Dropping down with his belly to the ground, his head thrust forward, he crawled to the corner. He peeked around, his nose lifting slightly as he sniffed the air. He stood then, tail still between his legs, and walked into the opening. He turned and looked back at Ned.

'Gone, huh?' Ned acknowledged. He slapped his leg with his left hand to beckon the dog back to him. He came at once, sat on the ground beside him and looked up at him.

'Good boy,' Ned affirmed, rubbing the dog's head and scratching his ears.

'Who you shootin' at, Sheriff?'

'Howdy Paul,' Ned greeted the man who had walked up to him. 'I thought the town marshal was supposed to make this a fine, safe town. Here I ride into town and somebody puts a hole through my perfectly good hat.'

As he spoke he held out his hat toward the marshal, his finger poking through the hole that hadn't been there when he arrived in town.

'Must be someone from out in the county,' Paul assured him with a straight face. 'I wouldn't have nobody in town here that'd do that. Close call, though.'

'Too close,' Ned agreed. 'Walk over to the livery barn with me an' I'll tell you about the rest of it. Then I'm headin' for the Rockin' R for a day or two. I'll be back here in a few days.'

5

'I really shouldn't be out here with you. Alone, I mean.'

'Why not? It isn't as though I'm some rogue you should fear.'

Nellie Henry glanced at her companion, then looked away. She glanced back at their horses, wishing she hadn't agreed to walk along the creek. 'It's not that I'm afraid of you, Leo. It's just that . . . it just doesn't seem like . . . I mean it wouldn't look right if somebody came along.'

Leopold Milosevitch spread his arms and turned a complete circle. 'Now who in the world would be coming along here?' he asked, grinning broadly. 'Especially with the chill of spring still in the air.'

His reminder that they were totally alone, that nobody was likely to come by, made Nellie even more uneasy. 'I am seeing Ned,' she reminded him. 'I'm not sure he would approve.'

Irritation flashed across Milo's eyes, but he masked it quickly. 'Oh, come now, my dear. It isn't as though you are promised to him or anything.'

Until that moment she hadn't noticed that he had removed his bedroll from behind his saddle, and was carrying it, tightly rolled under one arm. He walked to the bank of the creek, amidst a large patch of early wild flowers. With a flourish he unrolled the bedroll and spread it on the ground. 'Come, lovely lady, and sit with me and admire the beauty of as fine a spring day as one could possibly ask for.'

As he spoke he walked back beside her and put an arm around her waist. With it he impelled her toward the waiting blankets without making it appear that he was pushing her. But he was pushing her, and she felt suddenly very threatened by his persistence.

She shouldn't have agreed to go for a ride with him in the first place. It had seemed innocent enough. He had ridden up to her as if purely by chance, just after she left the Rockin' R to go for a ride. The spring day was simply too gorgeous to be allowed to go to waste. Besides, there were some heifers with new calves in a meadow just over a mile from the house. She knew her father would appreciate her riding out to check on them.

It had seemed impossibly rude to refuse Milo's offer to accompany her. Besides, she had to admit she did enjoy his company. He was such a brilliant man, and could talk endlessly about almost any subject she chose. He could recite poetry in ways that made her heart flutter. He wasn't as tall or strong as Ned, but he moved with a fluid grace that betokened great strength and control. She felt safe in his presence, as if nothing in the world could fluster or surprise him, or be beyond his ability to deal with it.

She knew Ned didn't like her even talking with him. He would be furious if he knew they were out here along the creek together, so far from everyone.

She didn't understand what was between the two of them. Well, they had run against each other for the office of Fremont county sheriff. But that was just politics. That and a job. She wasn't sure Leo, as he preferred her to call him, needed a job. He always seemed to have plenty of money. Maybe it was from an inheritance or something.

Anyway, the name Leopold Milosevitch seemed almost regal. His bearing was regal too, she thought. It flattered her immensely that he showed such an interest in her. She thought he might actually be in love with her, but that was ridiculous. She was just a cowgirl, a hardscrabble rancher's daughter. She had nothing to offer a man with a name and bearing such as Leopold Milosevitch.

As he impelled her toward the spread blankets a sense of panic began to rise in her throat. She looked this way and that, hoping against hope someone would ride by. There was nobody.

She glanced back toward the ranch yard. It was nearly a mile away, with intervening hills that completely concealed them. No sound from here would reach even halfway to the ranch.

The trees and brush that grew along the creek isolated them even more. Their horses were tied among the trees. The clearing along the creek that had seemed so innocuous at first loomed suddenly as a preplanned location, too perfect and convenient to have been ridden upon purely by chance.

She looked sideways at Milo. The smile frozen on his face suddenly looked sinister instead of casual. The gleam in his eyes was hunger, not the warmth she was accustomed to seeing there. She had to get away from him.

At the same time she didn't want to appear like some scared schoolgirl. She was a woman. She could control the situation. She had no reason to fear this man.

She tried to swallow, and could not. They were no more than six feet from the blankets, spread in a way that now looked menacing, not inviting.

She whirled suddenly, spinning out of the grasp of his arm around her waist. It caught him completely by surprise, or she was sure she couldn't have escaped his grasp so easily.

He whirled toward her. Fire flashed briefly in his eyes. The smile remained pasted on his face. 'What on earth is the trouble, my dear?' he asked, his voice as smooth and suave as ever.

'I — I — I need to get back to the house,' she stammered.

'What on earth for? We have a great deal of time yet. There's no need to leave this lovely glen we have so recently discovered together.'

He reached for her, but she wheeled away and started walking swiftly toward her horse. Everything in her screamed at her to run, run to her horse and flee. She refused to allow herself to do so. She would not go running away like some frightened child!

He came after her, reaching for her.

She shied away to one side, leaving his hand grasping at air. His smile disappeared. He stopped, watching her hurry back to her horse. She tore the reins from the small tree they were tied to and leaped into the saddle.

Once in the saddle a sense of relief flooded over her. Her horse was the fastest on the ranch, and she could ride like the wind. There was no way he would be any threat to her so long as she remained on her horse. She kicked the mare into a run toward the ranch. The mare responded by sprinting for a couple hundred yards, then slowed to an easy lope. Nellie glanced back over her shoulder. Milo was just getting on his own horse. She allowed the horse to maintain the easy gait, but kept looking back over her shoulder.

Milo obviously sensed the futility of pursuing her when he missed his last grab for her. He spun around and stalked back to the blankets he had so ceremoniously spread out on the ground. He gathered them up without rolling them. He walked swiftly to his horse. Wadding the blankets he tied them hurriedly behind his saddle and set out after Nellie.

Almost at the ranch yard she slowed her mount to a swift trot, lest she appear to be fleeing from Milo as she arrived. She well knew how her father would interpret that, and she knew just as well the ferocity of his quick temper. She didn't want to get somebody killed.

As she rounded the corner of the house she spotted Ned, just dismounting by the front porch. Joy and relief flooded over her, dissolving all restraint. She leaped from the saddle and ran to him, throwing herself into his arms.

Startled and surprised are both words too mild for Ned's reaction. He instinctively wrapped his arms around her, returning the fervor of her hold, as she hugged him. She suddenly began to quiver, then to shake uncontrollably.

'What happened?' Ned demanded. 'Are you all right?'

'Yes, yes, I'm fine. I'm fine,' she

insisted, but she sobbed the words and sounded anything but fine.

Sam growled suddenly at Ned's feet. He looked where the dog was looking just as Milo rode into the yard. He noted instantly the wadded blankets tied behind the saddle, then saw the clamped jaw and tight lips on the man who was normally a perfect picture of suave grace and aplomb.

He grasped Nellie by the shoulders and pushed her to arm's length. 'What happened, Nellie? Did he . . . Did . . . What happened?'

Even as he tried to ask what he could not get asked, his hand dropped to his gun. Nellie grabbed his arm. 'Nothing happened. It's all right. I'm just so glad to see you, though! I'm so glad you're here!'

'If nothin' happened, how come you're ridin' in here on a run an' him with them blankets all wadded up like that?'

Even as she talked, Hank, her father, stepped out on the front porch. In a glance he sized up everything Ned had already seen. Like Ned, his first instinct was to drop his hand to his gun butt.

'What's goin' on here, young lady?' he demanded of his daughter.

'It's all right, Father,' she insisted. 'Everything is fine. I just got frightened is all. I really had no need to be scared. Nothing happened. Leo didn't do anything wrong. I just got scared.'

As he watched the reactions of both Ned and Hank, Milo had stopped some distance from the others. He visibly fought to regain his composure.

'Nellie and I had a most enjoyable ride,' he said, trying hard to sound calm and normal. 'I'm sorry she seems to have become alarmed at something. I assure you it was nothing I said or did that caused her to have a sudden fit of panic. I am quite relieved she seems much better now.'

Silence settled around them like a cloud enveloping a mountain top. It sat there breathlessly, as if the center of that mountain might erupt with the ferocity of a volcano at any instant. It was Hank who finally broke the silence.

'I ain't sure what's goin' on, Milosevitch,' he said, 'but I 'spect you'd best be ridin' outa here. If I find out you did anythin' outa line with my girl, I'll be comin' after you, though.'

'You'll be second in line,' Ned declared, glaring holes through the man who was already his adversary.

Milo opened his mouth twice to answer, but closed it again each time. Finally he lifted the reins and turned his horse, leaving the yard at a swift trot.

The three stood there watching him until he had ridden out of sight. Only then did they notice three of the ranch hands, each with a rifle in hand, turn and head back toward the barn.

'You wanta tell us what happened now?'

From her father's tone Nellie knew full well it wasn't a request. It was a demand. She took a deep breath. 'I rode out to go check on the heifers. I was just leaving, just over that little rise south of the yard, when Leo arrived. He offered to accompany me, and I saw no harm in it. He suggested we ride over by the creek, where he'd seen a beautiful patch of wild flowers. I agreed, and they were truly beautiful. There was a big patch of them, mostly purple, with some bright yellow ones scattered among them. It was so beautiful it took my breath away. We got off our horses and walked over there. Then I noticed he'd gotten his bedroll from his saddle. He spread it out beside the creek and asked me to come sit there with him in the middle of the flowers.'

'And you did?' Ned demanded, unable to keep silent any longer.

Nellie shook her head earnestly. 'No! No, I got really uneasy. Then he started, kind of, I don't know . . . he put an arm around my waist and . . . and it was like he was pushing me over there, but he really wasn't forcing me to go there, but it felt like he was even if he wasn't, and . . . oh, I don't know how to explain it. But I got scared. We were all alone there, and nobody could see us because of the trees and brush and things, and it seemed all of a sudden like it was a place he'd picked out and planned or something, and I . . . I just panicked, that's all. I just . . . just ran back to my horse and got on and headed for home.'

She looked up at Ned again. 'Oh, Ned, you don't know how happy I was to see you here!'

'He didn't try to grab you or . . . or nothin'?' Hank demanded again.

'No. Well, no. Not really. It felt like he . . . like his arm around my waist was going to be something I couldn't get away from, but I don't know why it felt that way. It just scared me. So I spun away from him really quick. Then he did reach out like he was trying to grab me, and I ran. I ran like a scared schoolgirl!'

Ned reached out and wrapped his arms around her, drawing her to himself. 'Dang good thing you did, if you ask me. I sure as sin would've had to kill 'im if you hadn't.'

She looked up into his eyes a long moment. 'Do you really think he meant to . . . I mean . . . Did I really have a . . . a reason to get so scared?'

'Of course you did! A woman's instinct is never wrong at such a time.' A woman's voice startled them.

All three whirled to see Adelia Henry standing in front of the door, arms folded across her ample bosom, lips drawn to a thin straight line. She addressed her husband as she pointed the direction Milo had gone.

'Henry Henry, if that man sets foot on this place again I want you to shoot him right between the eyes. Do you hear me?'

The ferocity of her outburst stunned them all.

'Mama!' Nellie exclaimed.

'Don't you 'Mama,' me,' Addie retorted. 'You know as well as me what that man intended. He's not the first smooth-talking Lothario to try to take advantage of an innocent girl. Had it set up real fine, he did, getting you off there alone where nobody could hear you scream for help no matter how loud you tried.'

Nellie shuddered against Ned, who still had his arms wrapped around her. He buried his face in her hair so nobody would see the emotions that contorted his face.

Emotions play inconceivable tricks on us at unexpected times. Ned raised his head suddenly, his face now contorted by a sudden and uncontrolled mirth.

'Henry Henry?' he exclaimed. 'Hank, I ain't never heard anyone use your first name afore. You mean to tell me your folks actually named you Henry Henry?'

The tension exploded out of all four of them. The dam of their emotions burst. Her whole body shaking with suppressed laughter, Adelia declared, 'That ain't half of it. His middle name's Henry, too!'

'Henry Henry Henry?' Ned responded, trying to suppress his own laughter. Then all four started laughing as if they'd just heard the most hilarious joke ever told. Tears streamed down their faces as they leaned against each other and let the laughter drain the wrenching tension.

As they slowly regained composure, wiping their eyes on sleeves, or, in Addie's case, a lifted corner of her apron, she spoke again. 'I mean it, Henry. If that man sets foot on this place again, you shoot him or I will.'

She turned and walked back into the house.

The words ran through Ned's mind again. *Get in line, Addie. Get in line.*

6

'COUNTY SHERIFF INCITES INDIANS TO WARPATH,' the headline blared in letters two inches high.

Incredulous, Ned swiftly began to read the lead 'news' item in the fledgling *Wind River Reporter* newspaper.

This newspaper has recently discovered the fact that the Fremont County Sheriff, one Ned Garman, intruded himself on to the Indian Reservation pursuing a man he presumed, without evidence, to have killed a man. Within the Reservation he ran the unfortunate individual down, deemed himself both judge and jury, then executed him without warrant, without legal process, and without mercy.

It appears that Sheriff Garman discovered the body of a sheepherder who was in the employ of the Palisades sheep ranch. According to our sources, he neither witnessed the murder, nor had any means of identifying the killer.

Not one to let details or legality stand in his way, our intrepid Sheriff set out in pursuit, following or guessing at a trail he presumed to be that of the killer. When that trail led on to the Reservation, where Sheriff Garman has no legal jurisdiction whatever, he continued as if his election to the office of Sheriff made him King of Wyoming Territory.

Well within the Reservation, Sheriff Garman came upon an individual making camp peacefully beside a stream. Whether he made his presence known to that individual or not is unclear. What is clear, is that the Sheriff shot the man to death, whereupon he fled the Reservation without either identifying the individual or even attempting to bring the victim's body back where he might receive a decent burial. He did bring the individual's horse and saddle, however, for which it may be presumed the Sheriff received a pretty penny.

We may now expect reprisals from the heretofore peaceful denizens of the Reservation, as they seek to retaliate for the inexcusable incursion into the lands they hold sacred, and within which the government of the United States has promised them autonomy. When unwary members of white society are murdered and scalped, when our wives are savagely ravished and murdered along with our children, we will almost certainly be able to look back upon this moment and recognize the source of the Indians' wrath. It will be a doubly bitter pill to swallow when we realize it is we, the citizens of Fremont County, who have, by our misplaced and poorly contemplated votes, elevated such a cold-blooded and irresponsible specimen to such a powerful office.

If ever there was a time for level-headed and clear-thinking men to rise up and remove a person from office for malfeasance of duty, that time is now.

Ned looked around at the dozen or so people closely watching him. Butch Osterman, the bartender at the Mountain Springs saloon, had handed him a copy of the paper as soon as he walked in. 'You might wanta read this, Sheriff,' was his only comment.

Some of the denizens of the saloon were watching with open amusement. Some faces reflected anger, but not the red-hot fury coursing through Ned. Some looked almost indifferent, as though watching a cow eat grass.

'Who came up with all this bull . . . ?' he demanded of everyone and no one.

'I reckon you'd have to ask Percy,' a middle-aged man offered.

Ned glared at him. He knew him as

Clyde Ross, owner of the C-Bar-L ranch south of Dubois. Nothing in his manner indicated whether he agreed with anything in the newspaper's lead article.

'Them newspaper men put pertneart anything in the paper they think will rile folks up,' a man Ned didn't know opined. 'The more people they make mad, the more people talk about it, and the more people buy newspapers.'

Ned stared at the headline again, his anger rising to the point of exploding. Abruptly he turned and walked out of the saloon, the newspaper wadded up in his fist. Three of the saloon's patrons rushed out to follow him, certain they would be treated to the day's entertainment.

The door of the newspaper office nearly flew off the hinges as Ned burst in. The door slammed against a wall and bounced back, nearly knocking down the man who was immediately behind him. He walked swiftly around the end of the counter, directly to Percival Foster, editor in chief and owner of the *Wind River Reporter*. He grabbed him by the front of the ink-stained apron he wore, grasping the shirt beneath and a good bit of skin along with it. He lifted the man bodily off the floor and slammed him against the wall. Two framed certificates of some sort fell from the wall and crashed to the floor.

'What do you mean puttin' this pack o' lies in print an' callin' it news?' he demanded.

'Ow! Ouch! You're tearing the skin off my chest.'

'I'll tear the rest o' your skin off an' nail it to the front door, you lyin' weasel. Where'd you get this pack o' lies?'

'I just report the news! I don't make it up,' the newsman insisted. 'Now put me down!'

'I can't put you down. You're already lower'n a snake's belly crawlin' through the slime at the bottom of a manure pile. Now where'd you get this pile o' bull?'

The small group at the door stood

grinning at the spectacle of the newspaperman pinned against the wall, his feet a foot off the floor. They were pushed aside as Paul Thurmond shoved his way inside. He paused briefly, then went directly to where Ned had the newsman pinned to the wall. 'What seems to be the problem, Sheriff?'

Ned glanced at him, then returned his glare to Percy, then looked back at the town marshal. He shook the paper in Paul's face, keeping Foster suspended against the wall with the other hand. 'Did you read this?'

Paul shook his head.

'Well read the danged thing! Read what this mealy-mouthed lyin' son of a rotten pig-lover put in this thing he calls a newspaper!'

Paul took the proffered wad of paper and smoothed it out enough to begin reading.

Foster cried out, 'Marshal! Make him put me down! This is assault and battery. I demand you arrest this man!'

The marshal ignored him, his brow

deeply furrowed as he began to read.

'Marshal! I demand you do your duty! Make this madman put me down!'

The marshal glanced up at him. 'Now just hold your horses,' he said with exaggerated calm. 'I need to figure out who's in the right here before I go issuing any kind of orders.'

The newspaper owner continued to sputter and protest, but was totally ignored. Paul scanned through the article much more quickly than the time it had taken Ned to read it. When he spoke he addressed Ned.

'How long you s'pose you can keep 'im pinned up there?' he asked, in a calm and conversational tone.

'Till the hide pulls off his chest or till he tells me who put 'im up to puttin' that hog slop in what he calls a newspaper.'

'Where did you get this information, Percy?' the marshal inquired.

'I don't have to reveal my sources,' Percy insisted. 'Freedom of the press,

Marshal. I have a constitutional right to publish what I please. I have my sources.'

'Well, it's a cinch you weren't there when any o' this happened, so where'd you get the information?'

'I don't have to tell you that!'

The marshal walked over and sat down in the editor's chair. 'Well, I guess we'll have to sit down and think about this for a while, then.'

He turned to the grinning trio who had followed Ned from the saloon. 'Would one o' you boys mind steppin' out an' gettin' us a pot o' coffee. It looks like we might be here a while.'

He turned his attention back to Ned. 'Oh, by the way, Sheriff, you might wanta switch hands after a bit. Even a bag o' hot air like Percy'll get your arm tired, holdin' 'im up there thataway after a while.'

'How about I just start lacin' 'im out till he gets a bunch more talkative?' Ned countered.

'Well, I don't guess I could OK that.

It wouldn't be lawful for me to let an assault on a domestic rabbit occur inside the town I'm supposed to keep the peace in.'

'How about a slime rat?'

An empty chair sat against the wall a few feet from where Foster still flailed in the air. Ned abruptly lowered him and tossed him into the chair. Foster hit the chair so hard that his teeth rattled. His head hit the wall and bounced off. His eyes went out of focus briefly. He groaned and put a hand to the back of his head.

'Now that's a whole lot more friendly,' Paul approved. 'I'm sure the newspaper will duly report that the sheriff politely provided a chair for Mr Foster to sit in while we chat about the sort of things that can rightly be printed as news.'

'I don't have to ask you what I can print in my newspaper,' Percy protested again. His voice had lost its truculence, and sounded more like a whine than a threat.

'If you want to operate inside this town, you do have to have at least a pretense of printing the truth,' Paul rejoined. 'Otherwise I just couldn't see my way clear to protect you from any irate citizen you slander. I'm sure you're aware of the number of newspaper men that've been tarred and feathered and ridden out of town on a rail?'

Foster's eyes widened. He looked back and forth from one lawman to the other, then at the trio of grinning men just inside the door. He turned his eyes back to the town marshal. 'You wouldn't let them do that to me!'

'Don't bet on it. If you print this kind of stuff, I'm more'n likely gonna be awful busy over on the other side o' town when folks come lookin' for you. Only they might just lynch you instead of the tar an' feathers.'

Foster swallowed hard; for what was probably the first time in his life he seemed at a loss for words.

The marshal leaned forward in his chair. 'Did you ever see a mob tar and feather a man, Percy? To get the tar thin enough to cover a man, they get it awfully hot. Hot enough a really tough man screams like a woman when it's poured over him. Then they quick dump all them feathers on him, and they stick in that tar until it's like a second hide. Then they stick him astride a pole an' haul him out to the edge o' town an' dump him off. I don't know which hurts the worst, straddlin' that pole or fallin' off it. I ain't seen a man that could stand up by that time, though. Then whenever and wherever he gets to, he's gotta get that cooled off tar an' all them feathers off. I ain't never been there when it got to that part, but I'm told that it's just about like gettin' skinned. More men die from it than don't.'

He stopped and let the silence deepen. Foster stared at him, his face gone ashen, his eyes bulging. After a long silence the marshal said, 'Now I do believe you owe the sheriff an apology, and I do believe you owe me and the rest of this town your word that you'll check your sources a whole lot closer before you publish anything like this piece of pig tripe again.'

Foster looked back and forth from one lawman to the other several times. Then he bobbed his head once. 'I'll . . . I'll remember that.'

'So who gave you this pack o' lies?' Ned demanded once again.

Foster shook his head emphatically. 'I can't tell you that. He'd kill me. I . . . I should have asked you for your side of the story, I guess.'

Ned swore and stamped out of the newspaper office as the trio of observers scrambled out of his way.

The marshal studied the newsman for a long moment in silence. He sat hunched forward in the chair where Ned had slammed him. His arms hugged his chest. He moaned softly. For a brief moment the marshal almost felt sorry for him.

I wonder how much hide Ned had wadded up with his shirt? he pondered silently. His chest must be pertneart skinned.

He stood. Aloud he said, 'You're a lucky man, Mr Foster.'

The newsman looked at him incredulously. 'Lucky?'

'Mighty lucky. You're alive. You don't deserve to be.'

Without another word he walked out, followed by the trio, who hurried back to the saloon to share their story. It would be the talk of Dubois for weeks.

7

Ned rode blindly, seething inside. Something in the back of his mind kept nagging at him to slow down, get his emotions in check, pay attention to where he was going. He was too angry to listen. When a puny little popinjay of a newspaper guy could attack his reputation like that with no consequences, the world had come to a sad situation. If he had said any of those things to his face, Ned knew he would have had a perfect right to beat him to a pulp to defend his reputation. So why would it be wrong to do so when he had put that stuff in print?

The more he thought about it, the angrier he became. He had released the man and walked out of his office because he knew he was on the verge of beating him to death. He couldn't do that.

At the same time he kept asking himself, 'Why not? That's exactly what he deserves.'

It was the height of foolishness for anyone to ride along oblivious to his surroundings. It was doubly so for a lawman. It was asking to be killed, pure and simple. *Ask and ye shall receive* can be applied to more things than prayer.

A short distance ahead of him a blue jay exploded upward with a sudden flurry of wings, scolding loudly. At almost the same time Sam growled softly. Ned's attention was abruptly brought to the present. His hand dropped to his gun. He reined his horse quickly into the timber at the edge of the road.

'What is it, Sam?' he asked softly.

The dog stood within the shelter of the trees, his nose lifted, sniffing the air. Whatever whiff of danger he had caught seemed to be gone. He kept looking in all directions for a long moment, then simply lay down, watching his master for directions.

Ned remained where he was, listening intently. Through the clear space the road provided he could see an eagle soaring in a slow circle high above. A squirrel chattered in a tree somewhere to his right, scolding against the intrusion into his domain. Nothing else moved.

He considered riding through the timber, but the snow was still more than knee-deep to his horse where the sun had no direct access to it. It was, after all, only a couple days shy of May. It would be another two months before all the snow was gone at this altitude.

He reined his horse back into the road and nudged him forward. Just as he did something slammed into the tree above and behind him with a loud thwack. An instant behind it the report of a rifle reverberated from a dozen directions.

Ned dived from his horse into the brush. That he had grabbed his rifle from the saddle scabbard as he made that leap was the result of a great deal of practice. As he landed in the brush he tucked his shoulder and rolled, coming to his feet with the momentum of his plunge from the saddle. As he did so, he lunged behind the cover of a large spruce tree. From behind its trunk he aimed his rifle at the spot from where he thought the sound had originated.

A cluster of rocks rose 200 yards ahead in a series of spires well above the trees of the surrounding forest. Even as he watched, he caught a glint of sunlight reflecting from metal high up along one of the natural turrets. He fired at the spot. He could see rock chips fly, even as the whine of his bullet's ricochet faded off into the distance.

He considered sending his dog to chase whomever it was from his vantage point. Almost as quickly as he'd thought of it, he dismissed the idea. It was too risky. There was too much of a chance the gunman would spot the dog and shoot him. He'd rather stay pinned down where he was.

He realized suddenly that the dog was gone. Instinctively he knew the dog had already decided to circle around the gunman on his own. He put fingers to his mouth to whistle the dog back to him, then thought better of that as well. That would certainly alert the gunman to watch for the dog.

He studied the cluster of rock pinnacles. The stretch of road beside him had to be the only place where a person in those rocks would have a clear view of the road. He backed deeper into the timber. Wading the snow, he hurried through the trees and brush, moving parallel to the road.

When he had covered enough ground to satisfy himself that he was beyond the gunman's line of sight, he returned to the road. Staying at the edge of the trees for extra security anyway, he looked back down the road. His horse stood where he had been when he left the saddle.

'Justus,' he called softly. 'C'mere.'

At once the horse started walking toward him, holding his head to one side to avoid stepping on the trailing reins. As he came alongside where Ned waited, Ned leaped into the saddle and nudged the horse forward, leaning forward on to the horse's neck to keep as low a profile as possible.

Almost at once the timber began to thin. Massive up thrusts of rock denied even the hardiest of trees a toehold. He reined his mount in before he left the cover of the last of the trees, studying the rocky crags intently.

He had to cover 300 yards of mostly open, rocky ground before he could regain the cover of timber. If the gunman was still there, he would be an easy target the whole time.

'Where the Sam Hill is that dog?' he muttered.

As if in answer, Sam emerged from among the rocks and trotted halfway to his master. He sat down there in the middle of the road, watching Ned.

'I guess that means whoever was

there's long gone,' Ned surmised, urging his horse forward.

At the base of the granite needles Ned at once spotted a series of ledges and crags that made an easy ascent halfway to the top. He dismounted and followed it upward.

At a broad ledge he stood straight and looked down. A stretch of the road he had been following lay in clear view. 'Perfect spot for an ambush,' he muttered. 'Good thing he didn't allow for me bein' so far below him. He just plumb overshot me.'

Realization of how close he had come to instant death left him cold. He shook his head and fought off the feeling. As he started back down he noticed the bright brass of a shell casing. He picked it up. 'Thirty-thirty,' he noted. 'That sure don't tell me much.'

He debated pursuing his would-be killer. 'Well, at least we can find out what direction he went,' he decided.

He walked back to his horse and mounted. 'Track 'im, Sam,' he ordered.

Instantly his dog began to wend his way through the rocks. Without being directed, Justus began to pick his way cautiously through the rocks, following the canine leader.

Just as the ground leveled off Ned spotted the trampled grass and broken branches where a horse had been tied up for a while. He reined in and studied the area carefully for several minutes.

'Didn't wait long,' he muttered. 'Must've known when I'd be comin' along, knew where the best spot would be to take a crack at me, and rode here just in time to get set for me.'

A cold chill ran down his back. It had been far, far too easy. 'Gettin' that mad pertneart got me killed,' he scolded himself.

He lifted the reins. His dog sat still, waiting orders to continue. He received them at once. 'Go ahead, Sam. Track 'im.'

The dog whirled and started off at a swift trot. Ned marveled as he always did at the dog's uncanny ability to follow a scent. 'Dang shame I can't smell that good,' he mused. 'On the other hand, I ain't never understood how a critter that can smell that good can go an' roll in somethin' that's been dead for a week or two, an' think he smells good now.'

The trail the dog followed led in an almost direct line back to Dubois. It skirted all the heavy stands of timber, where the snow still lay deep. It avoided all contact with the road. But it was quick and direct. 'Whoever it is sure knows the country,' Ned observed. 'He had to've been watchin' me, an' he knowed just exactly where he was goin' afore he left town.'

As they approached Dubois the trail led on to the road that became Dubois's main street less than half a mile later. There Sam tacked back and forth several times, clearly losing the scent, then finding it, then losing it again. Ned called him off. 'C'mere, Sam,' he called. 'There ain't no sense tryin' to follow it any further. Whoever it was came back into town. Maybe you'll remember the scent the next time we run into 'im.'

He wheeled his horse and retraced his previous route, heading south. He crossed North Fork Creek, running bank-high with snow melt. He wrapped his legs around the saddle horn as they went over. He knew the water was cold enough to make his feet and legs ache for an hour if he let them drag in it. On the far bank horse and dog shook themselves to get rid of as much of the icy liquid as possible, then continued on as if it didn't bother them at all.

When he came to Dix Creek he turned upstream instead of crossing. The sun had already dropped behind the Teton Range, and the temperature was falling rapidly. He found a spot far enough from the noise of the rushing creek to hear other sounds, and made camp for the night.

Daylight found him back in the saddle. He swam his horse across Wind River, once again careful to keep his feet and legs dry. He also lifted his rifle out of the scabbard and held it across his legs, so the end of the barrel wouldn't get wet.

As he rode, the climbing sun baked away layers of anger and frustration, and a sense of joy began to creep through him. 'Well, maybe it ain't the sun doin' it,' he admitted to himself at last. 'The sun helps, though.'

Mostly his spirits lifted with each mile because he was that much closer to the Rockin' R Ranch. He had seen Nellie three days ago. It just seemed longer. He hadn't been sure how strong her feelings were for him until that last visit. It had been upsetting, to be sure. But she was OK. As long as she was unharmed, he'd opt for that kind of being upset any day of the week and twice on Sunday.

As he thought of it, he remembered the feel of her clinging to him, her whole body pressed against him, all pretense of poise and restraint gone in the sudden joy of his being there when she was so frightened.

'Might have to find a herd o' bobcats, just to scare her again,' he chuckled.

His reverie was interrupted by a distant rifle shot carried on the breeze.

Sam woofed his alarm.

'I heard it,' Ned responded.

Another followed, then two more in rapid succession. 'Good mile off,' Ned opined. 'We best be findin' out what's goin' on now.'

He kicked his horse into a swift gallop, standing tall in the stirrups in order to see as far ahead as possible. Nearly a mile later he approached a long ridge that ran east and west. He slowed his horse. The sporadic sound of rifle shots continued, but much closer.

As he neared the top of the rise he removed his hat. Riding just far enough to see over the top of the rise, he surveyed the area below. He couldn't have chosen a more opportune position. To his right two men had taken shelter in a cluster of boulders. One horse lay dead on the ground near by. A second horse stood to the west of the men.

To his left two other men were positioned behind a hogback that led out from a high embankment. They were lying prone, using the top of the hogback as a steady for their rifles. From a saddle-bag Ned pulled out a telescope. He dismounted, lifted his rifle from its scabbard, then crawled to the top of the ridge. Sam crawled alongside him, as if imitating his master.

At the top Ned extended the telescope and scanned the scene before him. The two men lying on the hogback he didn't know. Their horses were tied in a small grove of trees, and he couldn't discern their brands.

Swinging the telescope the other way he clearly read the Rockin' R brand on the standing horse. The dead horse lay on the wrong side for his brand to show. Ned recognized the two men pinned down by the others' fire.

'That's Wink an' Jim!' he muttered.

He laid the telescope aside and levered a shell into the chamber of his rifle. Steadying it with an elbow on the ground, he aimed a good foot above the nearest one to allow for the more than 300 yards distance. He fired, and saw the dirt kick up inches from the man's head.

Both men jerked their heads up and looked his way. He fired again, more to announce his presence than in hopes of hitting either of them. His bullet spewed dirt and grass just short of the nearer man.

Both men leaped to their feet and sprinted toward their horses. The instant they jumped up, both of the cowboys fired. One of the gunmen threw up his hands and flopped to the ground. The other one continued to run. Ned sent another round in pursuit of him, knowing he was well out of effective range. Because of the hogback, neither of the Rockin' R cowhands could any longer see the fleeing bushwhacker.

In less than a minute the man broke

free from the copse that had sheltered his horse, mounted and ran full tilt to the east.

Ned stood up. He removed his hat and waved it at the besieged pair. They responded by standing and waving back.

He returned to his horse, replaced his telescope, put his rifle back in the scabbard and mounted. He walked his horse down the hill to where the two awaited his arrival.

'You're a sight for sore eyes,' Wink called as he neared them.

'Run into a bit o' trouble, did you?'

'Dirty skunks shot my horse out from under me,' Jim moaned.

'You're lucky. I'm guessin' they wasn't aimin' at the horse.'

Jim nodded. 'He tossed his head just as the bullet hit 'im. If he hadn't, I'd have got it right in the gut, sure's sin.'

'Who were they?'

'Don't have any idea.'

'Let's go have a look.'

'I ain't got a horse.'

'One of 'em ain't gonna be usin' his.'

'I thought I hit 'im! Then he dropped outa sight, so I wasn't sure.'

'You got 'im. I ain't seen 'im move. I could still see 'im till I was almost here.'

Wink walked to his horse, mounted and rode beside Ned. Jim walked along behind. When they reached the fallen gunman, they dismounted. They turned him over. 'Know 'im?' Wink asked.

Ned shook his head. 'Can't say as I've seen 'im afore. Two gun man. I ain't seen anyone wearin' two guns for a long time.'

Kneeling on the ground, Ned went through the man's pockets. He found a derringer in one pocket and a short barreled forty-one caliber Colt in the other. He laid the man's rifle, the two holstered pistols and the two hideout guns on the ground. 'Packed a whole arsenal along with himself, didn't he?' Wink marveled.

'Where'd all them guns come from?' Jim asked, just catching up to arrive on the scene.

'The one you plugged was packin' all of 'em,' Wink said.

'You're kiddin' me!' Jim responded. 'Why's one man need that many guns?'

'Hired gun or an outlaw,' Ned offered. 'The only calluses on them hands are from thumbin' hammers an' drawin' guns.'

Both cowboys instantly looked at the dead man's hands. They were soft and smooth except where the calluses Ned had mentioned of constant practice with the pistols. 'Danged if you ain't right,' Jim agreed. 'Them hands ain't been doin' no honest work lately.'

'Why would a hired gunman be tryin' to kill us?' Wink demanded.

'That ain't half of it,' Ned responded. 'If I ain't mistaken, that horse tied up yonder's an Indian pony.'

Both men's eyes jerked up to the horse now clearly visible, still tied in the small grove of trees. It bore a saddle and bridle, but it was clearly marked with dyes the Indians used to identify their horses.

'I'll lay you three to one he ain't shod.'

'Indians never shoe their horses.'

'These guys ain't neither one of 'em Indian.'

Ned leaned across his saddle, his forearms resting on it. He looked back and forth between the two cowboys. After some moments he said, 'Well, it seems plumb obvious, but if you'da told me this a month ago I'd have told you that you were nuts. I'm guessin' they stole them horses from over on the reservation, left their horses there, rode over here just to kill a couple people. Wouldn't have made any difference who. Once they'd killed you, they'd have scalped you, took anything that Indians would be likely to take, and rode back to the reservation. They'd have been careful to leave a real good trail, so anyone that's half a tracker would notice the horses wasn't shod. That'd prove to anyone that it was Indians what done it. Once back on the reservation they'd have caught up their own horses an' hightailed it outa there.'

Both cowboys stared at him, mouths agape, trying to find a hole in his logic. At last Wink said, 'But why? Why would anyone wanta stir up trouble with the Indians?'

'Same reason someone seems hell-bent on killin' me,' Ned responded.

'And why's that?'

'Danged if I know.'

He didn't know. It made no sense. But he had a hunch he'd better get it figured out pretty quick, or he was going to be just as dead as the gunman at his feet.

8

'What happened to your horse?'

Not one of the trio was surprised at the rancher's first question. He didn't ask why the sheriff was riding into the yard with two of his hands. He didn't ask where the piebald horse came from that one of those hands was riding. He didn't ask, 'What happened?' He asked, 'What happened to your horse?'

'He got shot,' Jim Kneip answered. He knew his boss wanted the whole story. It just irritated him that his first concern was for the horse.

'Who shot 'im?'

'Don't know.'

Hank Henry glared holes through his hired hand for a long moment. He took a deep breath. 'Well, I guess that about answers all the questions a man could ask.'

Wink Phillips decided he should

jump into the conversation to head off an impending clash. 'We got shot at, plumb outa the blue, Hank. They missed, sorta. Got Jim's horse. We ducked down behind some rocks an' started shootin' back.'

'They? How many of 'em?'

'Two.'

'So what happened?'

Jim swallowed his irritation and got back into the conversation. 'We had 'em corralled behind a hogback, right by a little bunch o' trees, an' they had us pinned down behind the rocks. Ned here rode up to see what all the shootin' was about. When he opened up they up an' ran.'

'I didn't have a clear shot,' Wink excused himself quickly, 'but Jim dropped one of 'em.'

'This here's his horse,' Jim offered.

'That's an Indian horse,' Hank declared. 'He ain't shod an' it don't look like he's ever had 'is hoofs trimmed or ever seen a curry comb.'

'It wasn't an Indian,' Ned spoke up

for the first time, 'but they obviously wanted to make it look like it was. I'm guessin' they stole a couple horses over on the reservation, meant to kill someone, likely scalp 'em, then ride back over to the reservation and get their own horses back. That way everyone'd think it was Indians.'

Hank looked at each of the trio in turn, finally focusing on Ned. 'Did you know either of 'em?'

Ned shook his head. 'Never saw either one before.'

'Gunfighters,' Wink declared.

'What makes you say that?'

'The one I shot had a rifle, two forty-fives holstered, and two other guns in his pockets. Workin' cowpokes don't generally pack half a dozen guns around with 'em,' Jim declared emphatically.

'Five,' Wink corrected.

'OK, five. That's danged near half a dozen.'

'Three more'n a cowboy needs.'

'Five more'n he needs now.'

'So what'd you do with 'im.'

'Left him. Didn't have an extra horse to pack 'im out with. Ground's still froze up there, so we couldn't bury 'im. 'Sides, we didn't happen to have shovels with us.'

''Tain't right to just leave a man lyin', even if he was a gunfighter.'

Jim's jaw muscles bulged as his teeth clenched again. He took a deep breath. 'Tell you what, boss. Once the ground's thawed out we'll ride back up there with a shovel an' bury what's left.'

Wink stifled a harsh laugh so it sounded more like a snort. He looked away quickly.

Hank's face reddened. He clearly didn't like what seemed like insolence from one of his hands. At the same time he understood the men had nearly been killed and had a right to be on edge.

A fortuitous squeal abruptly broke the tense exchange. 'Ned! I didn't see you ride in!' Nellie ran from the house. Ned just had time to step to the ground when she ran into his arms. 'I didn't know you were coming back so soon!'

She glanced around at the other two. Before Ned had a chance to reply, she said, 'Jim! What happened to your horse?'

All four men broke into laughter. Nellie looked around at each in turn, her brow furrowed, her mouth slightly open. 'What was funny about that?' she demanded.

Hank recovered the quickest. 'The boys was all put out 'cause that's the first thing I asked,' he explained. 'We pertneart had words over that. Then you come out, an' danged if that wasn't the first thing you asked too.'

'Like father like daughter,' Ned teased.

He watched Nellie as he spoke, staring as if drinking in every feature. She wasn't all that pretty, he realized suddenly. She was tall for a woman. She probably stood five-seven, maybe five-eight. Nice and slim, though. Odd, now that he thought about it, for her to have such dark hair, almost black, and those pale-blue eyes that sparkled like they had candles in them. Now that he thought about it, her nose was a little big, too. She sure had nice lips, though. Even as he thought about it, he remembered the taste of those lips. It was all he could do to restrain himself from refreshing his memory, even though he knew it would mortify her if he kissed her right in front of everyone.

Her words brought him back from his reverie. 'So what did happen to your horse?'

Jim's anger was all pretense by now. 'That's all you Henrys ever think about. *What happened to your horse?* Never mind I got shot at. Never mind we shoulda both been dead, me'n Wink both. Just, 'What happened to your horse?''

'Your horse got shot?' Nellie echoed.

'See!' Jim crowed. 'Now wouldn't you think it'd be, 'You almost got shot?' But no! It's all about the horse.'

'Well, I can see you didn't get shot!' Nellie exclaimed. 'What happened?'

Wink repeated the story. Nellie

looked up at Ned with a look in her eyes that approached worship as Wink recounted how Ned had heard the shots and ridden to their rescue.

'That just doesn't make any sense,' Nellie protested. She turned her head back and spoke directly to Ned. 'That doesn't make any more sense than somebody trying to kill you.'

Ned shook his head. 'I don't know what's behind it. I 'spect I'll find out soon enough. Either that or I'll be too dead to care.'

The prophetic ring of the words left them all speechless as they struggled for a response. *Quiet as a funeral, all of a sudden,* sprang up in Ned's mind. Just as quick was the inevitable question: *I wonder whose.*

The answer would reveal itself sooner than he thought.

9

Behind the red rage that coursed through him Ned felt a strange sense of having just lived the exact same experience he was reliving. A crumpled newspaper jutted from his clenched fist. He stormed into the office of the *Lander Leader.*

Wilson Ziegler looked up as the door slammed against the wall, rattling the window and nearly everything else in the office. Ziegler took a deep breath, wiped his hands on an ink-stained apron and approached the counter. His voice echoed a combination of resignation and dread.

'Good morning, Sheriff. I thought you might be stopping by.'

Ned stopped in his tracks. He opened and closed his mouth twice. Before he had stormed into the newspaper office he'd had an angry tirade already formed in his mind. The body language of the paper's editor made him hesitate.

Wilson spoke before Ned managed to collect himself enough to begin his oral attack. 'Before you get started, you're right.'

Ned sputtered a moment. When he could frame the words, he said, 'Whatd'ya mean?'

Ziegler took another deep breath. 'I assume you came here to give me what-for over the lead article in the paper?'

'You're dad-gummed right I did!'

'And you're going to lambast me for printing something on somebody's word, without taking the time or the trouble to check out the facts before I published it.'

His words confused Ned, but did nothing to placate the lawman's wrath. 'If you already know that, why in the Sam Hill did you print it?'

Ziegler held out both hands, palms up, in a gesture of resignation. 'I don't have a reason that'll stand up to any standard of journalism. I was given the copy right at the deadline to get it in the paper. I was assured it was factual and needed to be published. I scanned it quickly, and instantly realized it would spur a great deal of conversation, and hence, sales of the newspaper. I just let myself get too engrossed in the process of typesetting, printing and publishing to read it carefully, or consider its implications. After it was printed and out, and I sat down and reread it more carefully, I was appalled that I had printed it. For whatever it's worth, I'll print a retraction in the next edition of the paper.'

Ned held up the hand with the wadded paper, then lowered it, then raised it again. Finally he said, 'So who gave you this load o' bull?'

Ziegler shook his head. 'I'm sorry, Sheriff. I can't tell you that.'

'You can't tell me the name of a bare-faced liar that's tryin' his best to turn the whole county against me? You can't tell me who handed you the same dad-blamed hogwash he gave to the paper in Neversweat, word for word?'

'He provided the same copy for the *Wind River Reported*?'

'Word for word,' Ned affirmed. 'And it danged near cost Foster his hide. Then you go an' print the same pack o' lies!'

'Once again, I apologize, Sheriff. After considering it, I knew it was clearly partisan, and clearly in open conflict with your character. I sincerely wish I had not printed it.'

'Just tell me who gave it to you.'

Ziegler sighed heavily again. 'I can't do that, Sheriff.'

'And why in the Sam Hill can't you? Your memory that short?'

'When he handed me the copy he said he'd provide me with the information, and that it was all true and provable, and needed to be published. He said it was imperative that I not reveal who gave me the information. Without thinking I said, 'OK'.'

'You said, 'OK'.' It was a repeating of

a statement, not a question.

'I said, 'OK'. In other words, I agreed to his terms, without giving due thought to the fact that I was giving my word. Even so, I did give my word. I cannot go back on my word, as much as I wish I could.'

'Was it Milo?' Ned demanded.

'I cannot tell you that.'

Ned threw the wadded up paper on the floor and stomped out of the office. 'Danged newspaper people!' he fumed as he walked away. 'Worse'n Philadelphia lawyers! They oughta run the whole passel of 'em outa the country. Don't serve no more purpose than a boat in the desert anyhow. Just stirrin' up trouble, all the time. I'd sooner have flies in my gravy than a newspaper in town. At least a man can spit out the flies. Oughta tie up the lot of 'em an' throw 'em in the hog pen. O' course they'd just lay there an' rot. Too doggone rotten for even the hogs to eat 'em.'

He was still muttering as he stormed

into the office he shared with Zeke Hubbard, the town marshal of Lander. Testimony to the growing popularity of the area, it boasted a four-cell jail, separated from the office by a solid wall.

'Well, I would guess you read the latest edition of our stalwart newspaper,' Zeke surmised.

'That what you call that there ink-smeared toilet paper?'

Zeke chuckled. 'It is a shame to mess up that nice soft paper with all that ink, ain't it?'

Ned took a deep breath. 'Do you know that what he printed was exactly the same thing that no-account Foster printed in his paper, up in Neversweat?'

'You mean Dubois?'

'Yeah. Whatever it's called nowadays.'

'That paper said the same thing?'

'Word for word.'

'So whoever wrote it gave it to both newspapers.'

'Word for word.'

'Who?'

Ned shrugged. 'I shook Foster till his

tongue got twisted around his eyeteeth so bad he couldn't see what he was sayin', an' he still wouldn't tell me. Thurmond threatened to have him tarred an' feathered, an' he still wouldn't talk.'

'I don't s'pose Ziegler would either, huh?'

Ned took a deep breath, beginning at last to simmer down slightly. 'At least he apologized.'

'Ziegler did?'

'Yeah. Said he was in a hurry, an' just copied it word for word an' didn't even read it close till after it was printed. He said he'd print an apology on the front page o' the next paper.'

Zeke's eyebrows lifted. 'That's a first! But he still wouldn't tell you who gave it to him, huh?'

Ned shook his head. 'No. He said he'd agreed not to tell where he got the information before he realized what a pack o' lies it was. Wouldn't go back on his word. It's hard to fault a man for that, I guess. Not that he needed to tell me.'

'The name Leopold Milosevitch comes to mind.'

'Who else?'

The door to the office flew open. 'Hey, Marshal! We might have trouble.'

'What's goin' on, Stumpy?'

'Couple o' Indians is ridin' into town.'

Zeke frowned. 'What's wrong with that?'

'They're armed to the teeth, Marshal.'

'Aren't they always?'

'They're ridin' right into town.'

'Nothin' odd about that. The reservation's just a few miles over. There's a road that reaches all the way into town.'

'Ain't they s'posed to get their stuff from the Indian agency?'

Ned snorted. 'That depends on whether they want wormy flour an' buggy corn meal or not.'

Stumpy looked over his shoulder, gulped audibly, and disappeared. Ned walked to the door just as a pair of Shoshoni slid from the backs of their horses in front of the marshal's office. Ned stepped back, holding the door open, holding his hand in an obvious invitation for them to enter.

As they did so, Ned said, 'Deide-Haih. Baika Dugaaini. Welcome. Come on in.'

Zeke stood as they entered the office. Ned said, 'You boys have met Zeke Hubbard, the town marshal here, I'm guessin'?'

The two wordlessly looked Zeke up and down, with no indication of recognition.

Ned spoke to Zeke. 'Zeke, this is Little Crow and Kills At Night. They're reservation police. They're the ones I talked to when I tracked Weston down.'

Zeke frowned. 'Who's Weston?'

Ned frowned. 'I guess I ain't been back down here since then, have I? I forgot I hadn't told you. There's a whole bunch o' stuff went on since I was here last, I guess.'

'Sounds like maybe you oughta fill me in.'

Without preamble Ned said, 'Somebody bushwhacked Cletus Woodman.'

'Ingevold's herder?'

'That's him. I tracked the guy over on to the reservation. He went for his gun. I shot 'im. I sent up a signal. Little Crow and Kills At Night came along, and I told 'em why I was on the reservation. I took the guy's horse to Neversweat . . . '

'Dubois.'

'Whatever it is. A guy there recognized it. It belonged to a gunman that hung around town there for a while. Nevada Weston, he said his name was. When I left there somebody circled around and got ahead of me. Tried to bushwhack me. I never did get a look at 'im. Then on the way back I came on to two o' Henry's hands pinned down in a bunch o' rocks. I opened up on the guys shootin' at 'em. Jim Kneip got one of 'em. They was ridin' Indian ponies. The one that got away hightailed it for the reservation.'

'Why was they ridin' Indian ponies?'

'I 'spect to make it look like Hank's hands was killed by Indians.'

'Now it is one of our old women who has been shot,' Little Crow declared.

Ned and Zeke looked at each other, then at each of the Shoshoni. It was impossible to tell if they were angry from their impassive faces. 'By whom?' Ned demanded.

'We do not know. It was a white man. He waited on the hill above one of our villages until it was light. The first one to go outside was an old woman. He shot her from the timber, then left. As soon as some men could catch horses and go after him, he was too far ahead to catch. They tracked him until he got to the river. Spotted Horse is a good tracker. He will know the horse if he finds his track again.'

'Now why would somebody go clear over on the reservation, shoot an old woman, then run?' Zeke demanded.

Before Ned could answer, Little Crow said, 'It is the ones who try to make us go back on the warpath.'

'Sure looks that way,' Ned agreed. 'Did you boys come into town just to let us know about it, or you got other business here?'

'We have furs to trade for flour and corn meal,' Kills At Night explained. 'We have money, too, from the man you kill. From the store here we get food that is good. From the agency we get what the soldiers have thrown away because it is spoiled. Then the agent keeps the money he pretends to use to buy our supplies.'

'I talked to the United States marshal about that a while back,' Ned offered. 'He told me there's been a bunch of complaints, and he'll see to it that the complaints make their way to Washington. Sooner or later they'll get rid of that agent. But if you'd load up a bunch of spoiled stuff he gives you and bring it here, it'd help. Then you'd have people here that know what kind of stuff they're giving you to feed your families.'

'You would take the bad food to Washington?'

Ned shook his head. 'I can't take it that far. But we can see to it that the whole town here sees it, and knows it's spoiled food you're gettin'. Then they can write letters to . . . to the council that decides things like that. They can get rid of the agent.'

Little Crow looked at both lawmen for a long moment. Then he said, 'If they do not, there will be trouble. More and more of our young men believe we need to get rid of him ourselves.'

'That's what I'm afraid of,' Ned responded. 'Try to keep them from doing anything. If they kill the agent, that will be just what the ones trying to stir up trouble want to happen. Then they will bring the soldiers, and a whole lot o' folks are gonna get hurt.'

'It will not be easy to keep them from doing something. They grow angry.'

Ned felt chills up and down his back. The area was a whisker away from a bloodbath, and he was right in the middle of it.

10

'You again, Stumpy?'

The marshal's stare and tone of voice weren't just chilly. They would have frozen water that boiled over from the coffee pot before it hit the ground.

Stumpy seemed not to notice. 'You gotta come over to Beyer's, Marshal. Right away quick.'

'Them two Indians ain't tryin' to buy liquor are they?'

Stumpy shook his head emphatically. 'No, it ain't them, Marshal. They don't even try to buy nothin' in town. They know it's agin' the law. No, it's one o' them hardcases what's been hangin' around.'

Ned looked up from his own desk, noting the tightening of the marshal's jaw. 'What is he up to?'

'Well, there's two, actually. They're tryin' their dangdest to bait Billy

Pomerau into drawin' on 'em. He's doin' 'is best to ignore 'em, but they're gettin' under 'is collar. I kin tell. He's about to blow up. An' if he ups an' goes for 'is gun, he ain't got no more chance'n a snowball in hell. Them's real hardcases, they is.'

'Now why would they be tryin' to goad Billy into a fight?'

'I dunno, Marshal, but you better get over there in a hurry or there's gonna be a dead cowboy, an' nothin' you kin do about it, on account o' you know they'll let Billy pull leather first.'

The marshal stood and walked around his desk. Ned stood at the same time. Ned walked to the rack on the wall and grabbed a double-barreled twelve-gauge Greener. He opened the drawer beneath the array of shotguns and rifles and grabbed a handful of shells.

'I'll duck around and go in the back door,' he volunteered. 'Give me a couple minutes to get there.'

Zeke nodded. 'Thanks, Ned.'

He turned back to the old cowboy who usually worked as a flunky on one or the other of the area ranches. 'You'd best stay clear, Stumpy. I don't want anyone gettin' hurt if we can help it.'

He didn't need to say it twice. Stumpy scuttled out the door and disappeared. Ned was positive he would be peering through one of the saloon's grimy windows before either he or Zeke got there, however.

Ned shoved two of the shotgun shells, each loaded with double-ought buckshot, into the Greener and snapped the barrels closed. He walked swiftly across the street, between two buildings, and approached the back door of Beyer's saloon carefully.

He stopped before he opened the door, listening carefully. When he heard nothing he turned the knob, then stood to one side as he shoved the door open with the twin barrels of the shotgun. There was no response.

He stepped inside and moved to his left quickly, then stopped to let his eyes adjust to the dimmer light. He was in a hallway that led off in either direction, marked by a door every few feet. He knew each door led to one of the 'cribs' where the 'doves of the roost', as they were known, plied their ancient trade.

Almost straight across from the door he had entered another door opened on to the main room of the saloon.

He stepped to that door, keeping in shadow, and sized up the situation. Two rough-looking men he had never seen before leaned against the bar. A dozen feet away a young cowboy leaned both elbows on the bar, trying studiously to ignore the pair. From the near-purple shade of his face and his tightly clenched teeth, it was obvious he was near his breaking point.

Just then Zeke Hubbard stepped in the front door. 'What's goin' on here, boys?' he asked in a carefully neutral voice.

Both of the men who were hassling the cowboy stood up straight and turned around. In a move that was as nearly identical as two men could manage, each dropped a right hand to touch the butt of the forty-five that each wore, low and tied down. As they did, one of them took two steps to the side, putting enough distance between himself and his friend to make it difficult for a single assailant to target both of them.

'Well now,' one of them said with exaggerated courtesy, 'it appears we are being visited by a genuine lawman.'

The other man made no effort at the phony congeniality. 'Where's the sheriff? He's s'posed to be the one showin' up.'

Softly the first man said, 'Shut up, Fred.' To Zeke he said, 'You shouldn't have come by yourself, Marshal. You ain't no match for either one o' us boys, let alone both of us together.'

'I shouldn't need to be,' Zeke stated. 'I'm sure you boys aren't here just looking for trouble. I think it's probably time you stop raggin' Billy, though. I doubt if he's done anything to ruffle you boys' feathers.'

Both men tensed, as if on some signal only they perceived. It was the first of the pair who spoke once again.

'Well, Marshal, if you think you're man enough to make us leave 'im alone, let's just see you try.'

When Zeke first walked in the door and spoke, as all eyes turned to him Ned had stepped inside the main room. He noticed at once the man against the far wall who stood up from a table, his back to the wall, a gun in his hand. As the speaker of the other pair challenged Zeke, the man outside Zeke's field of vision raised the gun.

He hadn't got it leveled when a blast from Ned's shotgun slammed him back against the wall. The roar of the shotgun in the confines of the saloon was deafening.

Both of the pair facing the marshal jerked their guns from their holsters. One of them whirled toward the sound of the shotgun. The other one grunted and took a step backward, as a bullet from Zeke's gun slammed into him.

At almost the same instant the one who whirled toward Ned doubled over and fell in a twisted heap on the sawdust-covered floor. His companion dropped to his knees, his gun slipping from fingers that refused to maintain their grip. He fell face down across his companion.

Ned broke the shotgun open, ignoring the spent casings that flew out and landed somewhere behind him. He jammed two fresh loads into it and slammed it shut again. All the while his eyes kept sweeping the room, watching for any more threats. There were none.

Nobody spoke. Zeke opened the cylinder of his forty-five and ejected the spent brass. He replaced it with a fresh load from his cartridge belt. Like Ned, he kept searching the faces of those in the room, assuring himself the threat was over.

He holstered his gun and turned to the bartender. 'You know these boys, Vince?'

Vince Beyer shook his head, his hands spread flat on the bar. 'Never saw 'em before today, Marshal. They hadn't been in here fifteen minutes before they started pickin' on Billy, though.'

Zeke turned toward the young cowboy. 'You know 'em, Billy?'

Billy shook his head. 'I never saw 'em before either, Marshal.'

'You don't know why they were on your case?'

'No idea. They for sure wanted me to pull leather on 'em, so they could kill me an' call it self-defense. I figured that out in a hurry. I ain't no gunfighter, Marshal. I'm just a cowboy.'

'You're a smart cowboy,' Zeke offered. 'A man that can keep his temper under control is a whole lot more man than one that gets himself killed 'cause he can't.'

The marshal turned back to Ned. 'This deal was set up for you.'

'I heard what he said,' Ned confirmed. 'Someone sure does want me dead.'

He was just as certain that whoever it

was kept getting closer to success all the time. And he still had no least idea who or why.

11

'You got a minute, Sheriff?'

Ned stifled the urge to throw something at the face poking through his office door. He took a deep breath. 'Don't tell me, Ziegler, let me guess. You're workin' on a story for your newspaper about how I spend my spare time kickin' dogs, shootin' stray cats, kidnappin' little kids, cuttin' 'em up in pieces, an' feedin' 'em to my dog.'

'Well, I didn't know the part about your dog,' Wilson Ziegler replied with a perfectly straight face. 'That's why I need to talk to you, so I can get the story straight in the paper.'

Ned glared at the newspaperman, not in the least mollified by the other's attempt at wit. 'Whatd'ya want?'

'I, uh, have some information that I'm reluctant to share with you, but at the same time less than comfortable in keeping from you.'

'Now that's a switch. I thought I was the one you couldn't give any information.'

Ziegler walked on into the office and shut the door behind him. He glanced at the door leading to the area where the jail cells were. 'Is there, uh, anybody in jail?'

Ned frowned. His curiosity was at least piqued. He shook his head. 'Ain't nobody here but you'n me an' the bedbugs.'

Ziegler nodded his head once in satisfaction. He pulled a chair over close to the sheriff's desk and sat down, leaning forward toward the lawman. Ned resisted the urge to push back away from him.

In a low voice, scarcely more than a whisper, he said, 'I have come by some information that may shed a great deal of light on the things that have been going on.'

Ned simply stared at the man, waiting.

'I, uh, well, I grew quite curious about an individual who has been hanging around town for nearly two weeks now, with no apparent purpose or connection.'

'The pilgrim,' Ned responded.

Ziegler nodded. 'You've noticed him, too.'

'I've seen him over at Beyer's. Seems harmless enough.'

'That's where he seems to spend most of his time. He also seems inordinately curious about the places in the area that have been homesteaded.'

'He could get that information down in Laramie, if that's what he wanted to know.'

'He could get the information about any of the places that have been filed on. He wouldn't be able to tell from that whether there were people who were actually living on their claim, in the process of proving up on them, that sort of thing.'

'Why would anyone want to know that?'

Ziegler edged a little closer. 'Precisely

my question. Why would this well-dressed, obviously well-educated individual have so much curiosity about such things in an out-of-the-way place like this?'

'It don't make much sense.'

Ziegler looked around behind himself, as if assuring himself there were no other people listening. 'I do, from time to time, engage in what some might deem nefarious methods of garnering information. I asked one of my, ah, sources, to find out that information.'

'Who do you have runnin' around snoopin' for you?'

'I would rather not reveal that.'

Ned's eyes flashed fire. 'I am sick plumb to death o' hearin' you say that! If you want me to listen to the rest o' this long-drawn-out tale you're weavin', I gotta know where the information's comin' from. If you can't trust me that far you can just haul your hind end out that door.'

The newsman took another deep breath. He glanced over his shoulder again. 'I will give you that information if you swear you will not divulge it. It is one of my best sources of information, and I absolutely do not want it compromised.'

Ned pondered it for several seconds, then said, 'Fair enough.'

'Very well. Are you acquainted with Lily Mae?'

'Lily Mae who?'

'One of the, ah, soiled doves at Beyer's.'

'You mean that real pretty little dark-headed whore?'

'That's the one.'

'She's hooked up with you?'

Ziegler's face suffused red abruptly. 'She is not 'hooked up' with me. She is, from time to time, an excellent source of information.'

A hint of a smile played at the corners of the sheriff's mouth. 'Does your wife know about how close you an' this, ah, young lady are?'

The red deepened on Ziegler's face. 'My wife is fully aware that I use her as a source of information, and that I pay her well for doing so.'

'So how does she fit into this here picture?'

Ziegler struggled to regain his aplomb. 'As I said, I grew quite curious about this gentleman who was spending considerable time here, asking questions, listening to everyone's conversations, it seemed. So I asked Lily Mae to see if she could get him drunk, and if she could manage to do so, to, ah, do whatever else she might, to loosen his tongue.'

'I suspect she could make a man forget all about home, all right, given the right situation.'

'She is very good at what she does,' the editor confirmed. 'She exacted all the information I could possibly have hoped for.'

'So what did she find out?'

'The gentleman is employed by the Union Pacific Railroad.'

'The railroad?'

'The Union Pacific.'

'What's the railroad snoopin' around Buckroot for?'

'The name of our county seat is officially Lander, Sheriff.'

'Yeah, yeah. Next year it'll be Lincoln or Jefferson or Whistlebritches or who-knows-what. So what's the railroad lookin' for?'

'It seems that there are not one, but two contractors, who are seriously considering building a railway through here.'

'Through Buck — Through Lander? What for?'

'They seem to think that Yellowstone National Park is going to become more and more of a tourist attraction. The Union Pacific and the Oregon Shortline are both considering building a passenger service along a scenic route all the way to the national park. The Union Pacific would seem to have the advantage, inasmuch as they already have that mine spur built from Rock Springs all the way up to South Pass City. It would be quite feasible, financially, for them to simply continue that road, following Wind River most of the way, up past Dubois and on to Yellowstone Park. His purpose is to identify those from whom they would need to secure a right of way, and where they could build the road on government land instead.'

'He could find out who had homesteads at Laramie. Why would he need to be up here?'

'You are quite right, but the records at the capital only show what locations have homesteads filed on them, and what ones are proven up and deeded. It does not show what ones have anybody actively living on the property and in the process of proving up on them. Those people have property rights, and would need to be considered in the process of procuring a right of way.'

Ned's expression was blank. 'I guess that makes sense, but why do I need to know that? There ain't nothin' illegal about his wantin' to know that stuff.'

'Quite true, Sheriff. But it may explain a number of other things.'

'Such as?'

Ziegler hesitated only briefly. 'I may have been in the newspaper business too long. It may have made me unduly cynical. Nevertheless, when there are a number of seemingly disconnected but serious events occurring, my admittedly cynical mind starts looking for a connection.'

'What sorta things are you talkin' about?'

'Think about it, Sheriff. There have been two overt attempts on your life, of which I am aware. There have been two events in which an effort has been made to commit crimes — murders, actually, and have it blamed on the Indians.'

'How did you know about both o' them?'

'I make it my business to know as much about what goes on around here as I can. I am also aware of a recent murder on the reservation by a white person or persons unknown. It seems to have been a clear provocation, hoping to incite some sort of attack in revenge.'

'You know about that too, huh?'

'I did manage to visit briefly with the two members of the reservation police who visited our town recently.'

Silently Ned asked himself, *I wonder if this jaybird ever says anything without soundin' like some danged school teacher lecturin' kids?*

Aloud he said, 'So you think there's a connection between all that and the railroad?'

Ziegler nodded emphatically. 'I did not make the connection until a young couple who had homesteaded along the Popo Agie, just before it meets Sage Creek came through town.'

'The Carlsons?'

'That's the couple. They had everything they owned piled in or tied on to that wagon, and they were on their way to homestead land somewhere more amenable to farming.'

'What about their homestead here?'

'Someone had bought it out. Someone had paid them considerably more than a fair amount of cash for their property rights.'

'So they just up and left the county?'

'Not without regrets. They were very much in love with the county, and they had invested a great deal of work in the house they had built, and so forth. But they were afraid.'

'Afraid of what?'

'Both the impending Indian war, and the impending war between the sheep-men and the cattlemen.'

Ned stared at the newsman in disbelief a long moment. Then he said, 'What Indian war? What sheep an' cattle war?'

'The ones they were convinced are about to erupt.'

'Or that someone's tryin' to get started?'

'Exactly.'

Ned's eyes suddenly opened wide. 'Someone's tryin' to buy up property where the railroad's gonna come through, afore anyone knows about it! There ain't nothin' like an Indian war or a range war to make folks scared enough to sell out, lock stock and barrel.'

'Exactly. Either war would suffice just as well.'

Ned pondered the thought another long moment. Then he said, 'So how does someone tryin' to bushwhack me fit into that, Mr All-wise Newspaper Detective?'

Ziegler actually chuckled at the title. It was the first time Ned could remember hearing the man show any sense of humor.

'Think about it, Sheriff. Who else in Fremont County has enough connections all up and down the river, and also some solid friendships among the Shoshone? It is probably only because of you that neither the sheepmen nor the cattlemen have launched an attack on the other. It is also you, and the relationship you have with the Indians, that has caused them to refrain from retaliating. It is also solely because of you that everyone knows the pretended Indian attacks were not perpetrated by

Indians at all. You are a most trouble-some thorn in the side of whoever is at the helm of what seems to be a rather well-financed operation.'

'Well financed?'

'There seems to be no shortage of cash available to those who can be persuaded to sell out. The Carlsons are only one example. I know of at least half a dozen others who have done so or received generous offers.'

'That's gotta amount to some serious money.'

'That also increases the danger to you. As I said, it is largely you and you alone who stands between these nefari-ous schemers and their intended goal. You are in grave danger, Sheriff.'

Ned was already fully aware of that fact. The newsman's words seemed to deepen the yawning hole of peril into which his job demanded he walk.

12

'It don't feel right, does it, Sam?'

The dog appeared to echo his master's sentiments. His head and tail were both down. Instead of leading the way, as he normally did, he lagged behind. Every movement the animal made telegraphed his reluctance to go further.

Ned had followed the Wind River for a while after he left Lander. Then he had diverted toward the high country on the pretext of looking for sign of whoever had committed the wanton murder on the Reservation. In reality, it provided an opportunity for him to visit the Rockin' R, and spend a little more time with Nellie. He had actually, at last, mustered up the courage to ask her to marry him. She left no doubt of her enthusiasm for the idea.

Neither did her parents. Adelia Henry

had immediately set about planning the wedding. The first day of August seemed impossibly far away for both Ned and Nellie. Adelia insisted it was not nearly time enough for her to plan and prepare the kind of wedding her daughter deserved.

A couple weeks camping in Yellowstone National Park seemed the perfect honeymoon.

The two days at the ranch were a welcome respite from his official worries. The third morning he pried himself away and headed into the high country. Today was his second day away from the ranch.

He had felt it when he crawled out of his blankets that morning. It wasn't just that the wind was blowing. The wind rarely blew in Lander, but in the high country it was a different story. It seemed to blow all the time. Since yesterday, however, the wind had shifted. The temperature was dropping fast. He didn't think much about it at first. Sudden squalls and thunderstorms were common in early spring. By midmorning he knew it was neither a squall nor likely to rain any time soon.

Justus continually made uncustomary efforts to turn away from their route. Every valley that opened toward lower elevations he seemed determined to follow. He fought against the bit, tossing and shaking his head when Ned forced him back to the direction he wanted to go.

At one valley Sam actually left them, trotting rapidly along a deer trail that led downward. A hundred yards down that trail the dog had stopped and turned back to look at them, clearly inviting them to follow. Justus made several efforts to follow him, until Ned, in exasperation, swore and poked the faithful mount with his spurs. He thought for a brief moment that the horse was going to buck in protest, but he tossed his head again and returned to the path Ned insisted on following.

Sam returned as well, eventually, but he refused to trot ahead as normal. He followed along behind, head and tail silently shouting his displeasure.

By noon the snow began to fall. The wind had died down briefly, and during the lull they were pelted with huge flakes of wet snow. They increased in intensity until they obscured everything more than fifty yards away. Then the wind returned with a vengeance. It picked up the fragile flakes and sent them into spirals and whirls, making it more and more difficult for the travelers to find their way.

In another hour they found themselves in a full-scale blizzard. Even in the timber the snow was so heavy, and the wind so insistent that their visibility was severely limited. Every time they had to cross an area of open ground they plodded blindly, unable to see more than three feet ahead.

When another hour had passed it was apparent that the snowfall was no passing flurry. Snow was already three to four inches deep, and falling heavily.

Sam's sudden growl jarred Ned to full alert. His hand dropped to his gun.

They were in a stand of timber just thick enough to moderate the worst of the wind. At the very edge of Ned's field of visibility he made out two horsemen. He called out to them, 'Hey! You boys lost up here?'

In the swirling snow he didn't even see their hands streak to their guns. Above the whooshing of the wind in the pines he heard three quick shots, but none seemed to have come close to him.

He whipped the reins and nudged Justus into a thicker stand of trees. 'Stay here, Sam,' he ordered the dog.

Sam had already started to stalk the shooters. At Ned's command he stopped and retreated to his master's side, watching him for instruction.

Ned shrugged deeper into his heavy coat. He holstered the gun he didn't remember drawing. His right glove, he noted, was between his left hand and the saddle horn. He knew he had instinctively jerked his hand out of the glove and drawn his gun when he heard the first shot, but he didn't remember doing so.

'Now why d'ya s'pose they was so danged quick on the trigger?' he mused. 'Runnin' from somebody, sure's anythin'. That means they been up to no good. Well, storm or no storm, we best see if we can have a little chit-chat with them fellas.

'Track 'em, Sam,' he ordered.

The dog instantly moved forward, head ducked against the wind-driven snow. Following closely, Ned found their tracks quickly. He didn't really need the dog's keen nose at that point. The trail was clear, but filling with new snow rapidly. He had to follow quickly. The snow would obliterate their trail in a hurry. If he fell much further behind them, even their scent would be too deeply covered for Sam's nose to pick up the trail in such a strong wind. On the other hand, if they rode a brief distance and holed up where they had some cover, he would ride right on to them before either he or the dog knew they were there.

He followed the trail with everything he knew screaming warnings in his mind. He could only trust the dog to notice the horsemen before he was visible to them, should they be lying in wait. Within half a mile it was apparent that the two riders were less than sure where they were going.

'Gonna be ridin' in circles if they ain't careful,' Ned muttered.

He shrugged deeper into his coat against the increasing bite of the wind. He knew the temperature must have dropped thirty degrees or more since morning.

'We better find a spot to hole up or we're gonna freeze to death in this,' he announced to horse and dog alike.

He had no more than spoken the words when the wind around them suddenly lessened. The change was so abrupt and pronounced it startled him. His hand dropped to his gun again.

Ten yards further on he saw the reason. A cliff rose out of the timber a

dozen yards to his right. It rose about
twenty feet, then leaned back closer to
him as it rose further, leaving an area
thirty feet in diameter almost free of
both snow and wind. 'A man'd be
plumb crazy to pass that up right about
now,' he declared.

He started to unsaddle Justus, then
changed his mind. 'You'll be warmer
with that saddle on than off,' he
muttered.

He loosened the cinch so the horse
would be comfortable. He swiftly cut a
large bunch of branches from nearby
trees. Perpendicular to the cliff, he built
a wall with them by lashing them to
young pines that grew there. He swiftly
gathered as much deadfall wood as he
could find beneath the swiftly deepen-
ing snow. He knocked as much snow
from it as he could and piled it near to
the shelter he had built.

The force of the wind carried the
snow over the top of the cliff where
much of it fell into the still air in the lee
of the cliff. The ground next to the cliff

stayed almost bare, but thirty feet from it the snow began to pile in impressive drifts.

'Might take us till summer to work our way past the drifts, but we'll be just fine here for now,' Ned announced.

He removed the bridle from Justus, knowing he wouldn't wander far, even without the deep snowdrifts. With them, where they were so swiftly growing, no horse would get very far away.

He quickly built a bigger fire than he normally would have considered, and spread his bedroll beside it, close to the cliff. As he hoped, the air currents there carried the fire's heat directly on to the rocks of the cliff, heating them. Even after he went to sleep those rocks would radiate some heat back to him. When he got cold, he'd just get up and stir up the fire again.

He made coffee and fed himself and his dog. He put a bait of oats into his hat so his horse was cared for as well. As soon as he finished the oats, Justus began rustling what grass he could find where the snow had not yet deeply covered it.

'Wonder where them boys that shot at us are gonna find to hole up,' he asked the dog as he was drifting off into sleep.

The dog, already asleep, didn't respond.

13

Morning dawned clear, cold, and stunningly white. Even the highest branches of the pines drooped heavy with snow. Looking over the drifts that circled his little oasis, Ned could see half a dozen branches that were broken off by the weight.

The three inches of snow within the circle of his campsite bore witness that the wind had ceased before the snow had stopped falling. Now the storm had moved on, leaving a dazzling world of white and a temperature well below zero.

He stirred the coals of the fire he had stoked a couple times during the night, heaping on the last of the fuel he had gathered. Its roaring heat quickly drove the chill from his bones. As he thawed snow for water to make coffee, Justus nuzzled his hat.

Ned chuckled. 'Time for your mornin' oats, is it?' he asked.

Justus pawed the ground, rubbed his nose along a front leg, then nudged Ned with his nose again.

'All right, all right,' Ned groused with more irritation than he actually felt. 'You'd think a man didn't have a thing in the world to do but dig out some oats for you.'

He put a handful more oats in his hat than he usually fed the animal and held it out for him. In spite of his urgency in prodding his master to provide it, the horse seemed to take longer than normal to get it eaten.

'It's about time,' Ned grumbled as he put the hat back on. 'I 'bout froze my head waitin' to get my own hat back from you.'

Ned wiped a hand across his eyes. 'Sun's way too bright,' he complained. 'Hurtin' my eyes already. I'm gonna go snow-blind if I ain't careful.'

He picked up a burned stick from the fire's edge and carefully felt it, assuring himself it wasn't hot enough to burn him. He rubbed it on his cheek bones and all around his eyes, the charred wood making a black mask that covered the upper half of his face. Unable to see himself in the absence of a mirror, he picked up a second piece of burned wood and kept at it until he was sure the coating was adequate to protect his eyes from the dazzling sun.

'Now if somebody calls me a dirty scoundrel, I'll just have to say, 'Thank you,'' he muttered. 'But at least I hadn't oughta go blind.'

An hour later he led the way out of the protection of the high cliff. He picked the spot where the drifted snow was the most shallow. Leading the horse he waded into it, breaking a trail so the animal could follow. It took twenty minutes to work his way through the first thirty yards, through snow that was chest deep. All he could do was step as high as he could, push into the snow, back up a little and repeat the effort, managing little more than a foot of progress with each step. By the time he emerged into the lesser snow of the area beyond he was huffing and puffing as if he had run a mile or two.

Sam remained behind Justus, perfectly content to walk where both man and horse had beaten the snow down to a level he could navigate.

Ned took off his hat and used it to beat the worst of the clinging snow from his clothes. Then he mounted, turned the collar of his heavy coat up around his neck and ears, and said, 'Well, let's see if we can find any sign o' them fellas that was so quick to shoot at us yesterday.'

He let Justus pick his way, knowing the horse would work his way back and forth, staying where the snow was the least hindrance. In the open spaces, except for the side in the immediate lee of the timber, the ground was swept clean by the fierce wind. Along that lee side of each open glade, the snow was anywhere from three to seven feet deep. Ned knew the deepest of those drifts would take until late August to melt, at this altitude.

Once into the more open space, Sam had taken the lead. Whenever there was deeper snow they couldn't find an easy way around, he would drop back behind, letting the horse break the trail. Whenever they had to traverse an area of even deeper snow, Ned would once again dismount and lead the way, breaking the trail for his horse.

They had struggled along that way for nearly an hour when Sam growled. Justus stopped dead in his tracks without Ned needing to tell him to do so. Ned studied the direction the dog was staring for a long while before he saw it. A dozen yards to his right a hump appeared in the snow where a drift would not normally form. Sam was staring fixedly at it.

Ned dismounted. Watching all around, he walked over to it. He reached out a foot and swiped the snow away. A patch of hide and hair appeared through the snow. He continued to sweep snow aside with his foot until he was sure what he was seeing. 'That's a horse,' he confirmed. 'Still saddled.'

He looked around again, nervously. Kicking more snow off of the frozen animal he swore. 'He's still got somebody's bedroll tied behind the saddle! Now why would someone leave his horse when he gave out, an' not even take his blankets?'

Kicking more snow away, he said, 'Saddle-bags are gone. No rifle in the scabbard. The rider must've walked away carryin' the saddle-bags and rifle, an' no blankets. That don't make no sense at all.'

He mounted his horse again. He studied the dead animal, again looking all around for some clue to a scene that made no sense. After a while he said, 'Can you track 'em, Sam?'

Without the fierce wind the dog's nose seemed more than adequate to pick up the rider's trail. The dog started off at as rapid a pace as the snow permitted.

After he'd gone another 300 yards further he stopped again. Once again a growled warning alerted Ned as he did so. This time Ned was quicker to spot the incongruous hump in the snow. 'Another one!' he muttered. 'Gotta be them two fellas that shot at us. Rode their horses till they plumb gave out, then walked off an' left 'em. Now don't that beat all! What sorta fellas would do somethin' like that in this here country? Whatd'ya bet this one didn't take no blankets either.'

To satisfy himself he dismounted and kicked the snow off the second dead horse. There was less snow on this one. 'Been dead an hour or two less than the other one,' he mused.

As he suspected, the second animal still had the rider's bedroll attached, but only by one thong. The other had been untied. 'Looks like he started to take his blankets, but quit. I wonder if he just decided not to, or if his hands got too cold and he couldn't untie the knot?'

He looked all around again, a sense of being watched making his skin crawl. He knew it had to be his imagination. If he were being watched, Sam would have let him know. Instead the dog just stood looking at him, waiting for directions.

He mounted Justus again. 'Can you find 'em, Sam?'

The dog immediately whirled around and walked away. Ned followed warily. It was a little more than a quarter-mile away when the dog stopped once again. He growled once, then stood, staring into the trees.

Ned dismounted. He followed the dog's stare for a long while before he figured out what the dog was looking at. A chill ran down his back. He shuddered. Uncharacteristically he swore softly.

Twenty yards ahead was a dense tangle of dead wood and brush. Some long-forgotten storm had toppled a large tree that had taken a couple more with it en route to the ground. Brush had grown up in and around the tangle of branches, making an impenetrable patch of brambles. During the storm that tangle had provided almost as good a shelter from the wind as the cliff beneath which Ned had camped. The pair of riders had evidently found it and collapsed, exhausted, in its shelter from the driving wind. They would never leave that shelter.

Too lightly dressed for the weather, they were probably nearing frostbite before they stopped. They both wore low-crowned, flat hats that would have been at home in the desert southwest, but not in the Wyoming mountains. They wore gloves, but made only of thin kidskin. That would have been helpful in drawing the guns that both wore, low and tied down. They were almost as good as nothing against the cold.

Within minutes of sitting down, with no fire and no blankets, they would have grown too lethargic even to try to defend themselves against the weather. They probably lost consciousness before they even realized they were dying. 'They say once you get so cold, you don't feel it no more at all,' Ned muttered. 'You just feel plumb warm an' comfortable, an' go to sleep. I reckon it must be so. They look like they died plumb peaceful.'

The frost-covered faces of the pair were as expressionless as the bark of the frozen trees around them. A rifle and a pair of saddle-bags lay covered with snow beside each of them.

'I wonder what was so all-fired important in them saddle-bags they took them an' left their blankets?'

He sighed heavily, but stayed in the saddle. He studied the pair another long moment. He sighed heavily again. Still, he made no move to dismount.

Several minutes went by. Sam, sitting on the ground, watching his master, scooted closer without standing. He whined once. It was as close as the dog could come to saying, 'So do something!'

Ned's eyes dropped to the dog. He filled his lungs with the sharp air again, letting it out slowly. The dog whined again. 'Yeah, yeah,' Ned muttered. 'I know. Stop naggin'. I s'pose I'll have two of you naggin' at me, come August.'

He swung down from the saddle. He walked over to the pair and nudged the legs of one with the toe of his boot. It was like kicking a rock. He laughed suddenly and inappropriately. 'Now that's what I call a couple o' stiffs,' he said.

Somehow there was no mirth in the words — or the laugh either.

He kicked the snow off one pair of saddle-bags and picked them up. Their weight was startling. 'What in the world are they packin'?' he asked either the horse or the dog. Neither one bothered to answer.

Opening one of the bags he whistled. It was filled with money, both paper and gold, and jewelry. So was the other one.

A quick check of the other set of saddle-bags revealed an equal amount of obviously ill-gotten treasure. 'No wonder they shot so quick when I hollered at 'em,' he said. 'They sure enough robbed someone. A lot of someones, by the look of it.'

He secured both sets of saddle-bags on his horse, placing one set in front of the saddle and the other on top of his bedroll. 'That's too much weight for a long ride, ain't it, Justus? Can't help it, though.'

He stepped into the saddle. 'Well, that changes the plan, I guess. We'd best be gettin' down off this here mountain the first thing,' he announced. 'That sun's warmin' things up in a hurry, but I still don't wanta spend another night up here.'

He headed almost due east, as directly as he could, allowing for the draws and canyons where the snow had drifted too deeply for him even to try to navigate. As the day wore on the sun became warm on his face and the air lost its sharp bite. Shortly after midday he came across the trail of a herd of elk.

'Now that there's a godsend,' Ned

breathed. 'Now we got a whole herd o' elk bustin' a trail for us, an' headin' down outa the high country the same as we are.'

They made better time after that. As they worked their way lower in altitude, the amount of snow steadily lessened. When they came to Sage Creek they followed it, staying far enough away to avoid its crashing roar as it ran well over its banks already with melting snow.

They were a good 3,000 feet lower than they had started the day when they came in sight of the Doubletree ranch. The snow they rode in was a pretty consistent four-inch depth by then. It wasn't as difficult to navigate as the deeper snow up higher, but it was fatiguing to ride in, nonetheless.

Smoke trailed upward from the chimney of the main house, from the cook house, and from the bunkhouse. 'Already gettin' the bunkhouse warmed up too, looks like,' he commented.

He rode into the yard to the usual barking of the dogs. Sam looked after his requisite social sniffings and greetings as Ned rode to the main house.

Before he even got his horse stopped, Glen Durk stepped out the front door.

'Well, howdy, Sheriff. Get down an' come in. You look like you an' your horse are both wore down to a nub.'

'Evenin' Glen,' Ned responded as he stepped down and shook hands with the rancher. 'Yeah, it's been a tough ride today.'

'You get caught in the high country in the storm?'

'Yeah, we did for a fact.'

'Wonder you didn't freeze to death.'

'We got sorta cold,' Ned admitted. 'We found a pretty good shelter to wait it out in, though. It don't look like you got near as much snow.'

'Nah, we don't usually get nothin' like the high country does.'

All the while they talked, Glen kept eyeing the extra saddle-bags that burdened the sheriff's horse, but he didn't mention them. Instead he said, 'We got another visitor ridin' out the storm. He reckons to head up to the high country tomorrow, if the weather holds.'

'That so?'

'He'da likely headed out today, but I told 'im he oughta wait a day at least.'

'Why's he so anxious to head up there?'

'Lookin' for someone.'

Instead of answering, Ned simply looked at the rancher. While not actually answering the obviously questioning look Glen said, 'Why don't you go ahead and take care of your horse and come on in. The missus is fixin' supper. I'll tell 'er to throw an extra bean in the kettle. We can talk better once you get somethin' hot in your belly, I'm guessin'.'

It did sound like a fine idea.

14

'Pinkerton?'

The man across the table looked like he could have been half the Pinkerton Detective Agency all by himself. The man nodded, his mouth too full of food to respond.

By the time the stranger had finished the bite, Ned had filled his own mouth and was chewing busily.

Glen turned to his wife, swallowing his own bite. 'I don't think we're gonna get much out've either one o' them till they get their bellies full, Emma. I coulda just as well waited till after supper to introduce 'em.'

Emma smiled at her husband as she took a much daintier bite than any of the men were content to deal with. 'I guess that means they're hungry.'

'It means you're one fine cook,' Glen argued, pleased at the tinge of red that instantly colored his wife's cheeks.

She demurred with rather obvious pleasure at her husband's compliment. 'I think it just means they're awfully hungry.'

'Well, I hope so,' Glen rejoined. 'I'd rather feed a hungry man anytime than one that ain't.'

Emma frowned at her husband. 'Why?'

Glen pointed a fork at his wife to emphasize his words as he talked around another mouthful. 'Do you remember that mountain man type fella that stopped in last fall?'

'Oh yes. Jeremiah Henderson, I think his name was.'

Glen nodded. 'Well when I invited him to supper, he said he wasn't really hungry, but he guessed as how he'd eat a bite with us.'

'He told you he wasn't hungry?'

'That's what he said.'

'Why, that man ate everything except the last bite of food from every dish and platter on the table! I cooked enough food to feed our family and all four of the hands, if they weren't eating in the cook house. And he ate it all!'

'Except the last bite of everything,' Glen reminded her.

She giggled. 'I've seen people do that before. Somewhere it must be impolite to eat the last bite of anything, so he ate everything in sight except that last bite. He did use the last piece of bread. He used it to wipe every last speck of food off his plate. I could have put that plate straight into the cupboard without washing it.'

'That's my point,' Glen concluded. 'That's what it's like to feed a man that ain't hungry. A man that's hungry will get full after a while.'

As if to belie the statement, the stranger said, 'I could sure use seconds on them spuds, if you don't mind, ma'am.'

Smiling, Emma passed him the bowl of mashed potatoes. When he had helped himself to a second generous portion of them, she passed him the meat and gravy in turn. Ned followed suit, refilling his own plate. 'There's nothin' better'n elk backstrap, mashed taters'n gravy,' he asserted.

'This is elk?' the stranger questioned.

Glen nodded. 'Shot 'im out the front door,' he said. 'They come down outa the high country whenever the weather turns bad, or things get dry. Head straight for the river. One o' them keeps the kids eatin' for pertneart a week.'

The two children eating at the table raised their heads instantly. Neither had made a sound since the meal had begun. The girl raised a hand, as if asking permission to speak. Emma said, 'What is it, Eunice?'.

Eunice, all of four years old, looked directly at Ned. 'We don't really eat that much, Sheriff Garman. Father likes to asaggermate.'

'Exaggerate,' Emma corrected with a smile.

Herman, because he was the ripe old age of six, spoke at the table without permission. 'Pa says it ain't lyin' if you just exaggima . . . exaggarate.'

Uncomfortable silence followed the

remark for the briefest moment before Ned said, 'Well it sure ain't no exaggeration to say this is one fine meal, Mrs Durk. I may have to send my wife up here for a while so's you can teach her to cook like this.'

'Why, Sheriff! I didn't know you were married!'

Ned swallowed a bite of food hurriedly. 'Oh, I ain't, ma'am. Not yet. But I'm sure enough engaged.'

'The Henry girl?' Glen surmised.

Ned nodded enthusiastically. 'That's her. Nellie. I popped the question an' she sure 'nough said 'Yes'.'

'Now that makes a fella wonder at the girl's intelligence,' Glen offered.

'Well! When is the big event?' Emma asked, ignoring her husband's barb.

'First of August.'

'Wonderful! Are we invited?'

'Oh, sure. I 'spect lots o' folks will be there, the way Adelia started makin' plans the minute she found out we was official engaged.'

'I assume you will live in Lander?'

'Yes, ma'am. I done bought a house in Lander a while back. Been batchin' there when I ain't traipsin' all over the county.'

'If you're anything like my husband, I suspect the house could use a woman's touch by now,' Emma offered.

'You'll sure have to stop spittin' on the floor,' Glen declared.

'Do you spit on the floor, Sheriff Garman?' Eunice asked in obvious horror.

Everybody at the table chuckled at the response except Herman. He simply stared at Ned in wide-eyed awe. 'Do you chew t'bacca, Sheriff?'

Ned grinned. 'No, I don't chew tobacco, son. And no, Eunice, I don't spit on the floor. If I did, I think my ma would come back from her grave and use that wash stick on me again.'

'Your ma whipped you with a wash stick?' Herman demanded. 'My ma just uses one o' Pa's old belts. That's bad enough.'

'And I'll do it again, if you two don't

stop interrupting the adults at the table and eat your supper.'

Both children obediently returned their attention to cleaning up their plates. Everybody ate in silence for several minutes. Eunice raised her head suddenly, eyes wide. 'Did Papa spit on the floor before you trained him better, Mama?'

Nobody at the table was able to control the laughter that time. Eunice looked crushed that what she said had struck everyone so funny. Emma rushed to her rescue. 'No, dear. Your father was quite civilized before we were married. Now eat your supper.'

The rest of the meal was completed without further interruption. When Glen was satisfied the guests had eaten their fill, he said, 'Why don't we go in the parlor outa the way while Emma an' the kids clean up.'

As they stepped into the only other room that the house boasted Ned was impressed once again with the skill with which the building had been done. On one side of the room a sleeping loft provided a bed for each of the children, end to end, with a divider between. Below one of the 'upper bunks', a double bed was walled on both ends, with a heavy curtain that could be drawn across it for privacy.

From a shelf Glen lifted down a pipe. He drew his knife and ran it around the inside of the bowl. He opened the door of the pot-bellied stove and tapped the pipe against the edge of the door, so that the ashes fell inside the stove. While he had it opened he added a couple pieces of wood from the wood box that sat beside it. He packed his pipe from a humidor of tobacco that sat on the same shelf the pipe had occupied. When he was satisfied with the fill of his pipe, he picked up a slender stick from the wood box. Holding it into the fire he ignited the end of it, then used it to light his pipe. He tossed the stick into the fire, then closed the stove's door.

He crossed to a rocking-chair and sat

down. Leaning back, he took a couple long puffs of the pipe, then said, 'Well, John, I 'spect the sheriff has about a dozen or two questions he'd like answered. Then, if I ain't mistook, he's likely got a s'prise or two for you.'

John Hamlinson's eyebrows rose inquisitively, but Glen smugly studied the smoke from his pipe, refusing to respond to the unasked question.

John shrugged his massive shoulders. 'You're the Fremont County Sheriff, I have assumed,' he directed at Ned.

Ned just nodded, so John continued: 'Well, as Glen already said, my name's John Hamlinson. I'm in the employ of the Pinkerton Detective Agency. I am currently on the trail of at least five men who have committed a string of major robberies.'

'Two stagecoaches, three banks,' Glen interjected.

'Not to mention two trains,' John added.

'I didn't know about the trains,' Glen said, sounding apologetic.

'The Union Pacific does not like to have robberies of its trains advertised.'

'Bad for business,' Ned guessed.

'Precisely.'

'Who's behind it?'

'That's what I'm working to find out.'

'Any good leads?'

'An idea or two, but nothing I could take to a judge to get warrants on the basis of.'

'You know what any of 'em look like?'

'Only general descriptions.'

'Where'd all these outfits get robbed? It seems like I shoulda heard some about it.'

'Far enough away it was not suspected that any made their escape this direction.'

'But they did.'

'Apparently. Well, yes. We know they did. We finally got some leads, and following them has led me all the way up here.'

'Up here? That must mean the

robberies was down south.'

'The closest was Cheyenne. One was right on the outskirts of Denver. Several were in Kansas.'

'That's pretty spread out.'

'Not only spread out, but lucrative. They managed to abscond with a great amount of money, both paper money and gold, as well as some very valuable jewelry.'

'If they're pullin' all that off way down there, why are they headin' up this way?'

'That's exactly what I'm supposed to be finding out.'

Ned studied the big detective for a long moment. He stood up and said, 'I'll be right back.'

He walked through the kitchen and out the door. He returned moments later carrying two sets of saddle-bags. He carried them into the room and dropped them on the floor next to the Pinkerton investigator. They landed on the floor with a clunk that made the whole floor vibrate.

John sat bolt upright, grabbed one of the bags and flipped it open. He looked inside, then looked back at Ned, mouth agape. Ned sat back down and watched silently.

John returned to the saddle-bags and examined the contents swiftly. He lifted one watch and a necklace that were both very ornate, very expensive looking. 'No doubt about it,' John declared.

'Some o' the stolen stuff?'

'Absolutely. Where did you get these, Sheriff?'

With a perfectly straight face Ned said, 'Oh, I sorta found 'em layin' around up on the mountain.'

'I figured that out when I saw you take 'em off your horse,' Glen declared. 'What with John already bein' here, an' I saw how heavy they was, I knowed that's what they had to be.'

John opened his mouth twice, then closed it again each time. At last he said, 'There didn't happen to be some men rather close by, by any chance, did there?'

Ned decided it was time to stop tormenting the detective. Besides, it obviously wasn't upsetting him, so there was no point. He swiftly filled him in on the two riders he had glimpsed in the middle of the blizzard, their instant response when he had called out to them, and all that had happened after that. When he finished there was a long silence while John obviously sorted things into place in his mind.

'Just two?' was the next thing he said.

'That's all I saw. I didn't see tracks of anyone else. O' course the snow would've covered a trail in a hurry. I hunted a while afore I found those two.'

'Dressed like fellas from down south, you say.'

Ned nodded. 'Wore them sorta flat-crowned hats like guys do that hail from Nevada, Arizona, down in that country. Real thin gloves. Fancy vests, but real light coats. Didn't even have sense enough to wrap up in their blankets to try to stay warm. Just walked off from their horses after they rode 'em to death.'

Silence again, until John said, speaking softly, 'They had no idea how hard it is on a horse to ride 'im hard in high altitude, with a heavy load. No idea what to do if a storm catches you up there. They must have been riding up that high instead of following the river to avoid being seen by anyone. But they were still heading north. Now where in the world would they be going north of here?'

Glen chuckled unexpectedly. 'There is actually such a thing as north of here, John. This ain't really the north end o' the world, you know. The north pole's gotta be fifteen or twenty miles on further north.'

His sarcasm was lost on the detective. 'But what is there north of here that would attract men of that caliber, who already possessed the amount of money they were carrying?'

Ned had an idea, but he wasn't nearly ready to verbalize it yet. Instead he said, 'Well, I need to hole up for a day or so, to give my horse a chance to rest, if I can impose on your hospitality, Glen?'

Glen bobbed his head instantly. 'Of course. Glad to have you. Stay as long as you want. Of course I might put you to work helpin' the boys get hay to the cows till the snow melts.'

'Glad to help out, as long as you got a spare horse for me.'

He turned back to the detective. 'I'll be headin' back toward Lander — '

'By way of the Rockin' R, by any chance?' a teasing voice from the kitchen door interrupted.

Ned felt his face redden, but he grinned. 'Well, it's a long ride all the way to Buckroot from here. It just makes sense to break up the trip a little. Besides, my horse is bound to be pretty tired.'

'Well, that'll do to tell, Sheriff,' Emma grinned as she turned back to her work.

Ned turned back to the investigator. 'What I was about to say was to suggest you ride along with me, and we'll see what we can figure out. We can ask some folks along the way if they've seen any o' the other guys in that outfit.'

John considered it a long moment. 'Well, that's as good a plan as any other at this point. I'll be happy to ride with you, Sheriff.'

Ned stood again. 'Well, then, if you don't mind, Glen, I think I'll head on out to the bunkhouse and see if I can wrangle an empty bunk. I didn't sleep a whole lot last night.'

John took his cue from the sheriff. 'That does sound like a good idea. I'll come along.'

As they passed through the kitchen they thanked Emma again for the delicious supper, as if they had just graduated from Madam Primright's school of manners.

Both children, each with a dishtowel in hand, stared at them.

'G'night, Eunice. G'night, Herman. You kids sleep tight. Don't let the bedbugs bite.'

Both of them giggled as they returned to their chores. 'Sure be nice to have a couple o' them of my own, one o' these days,' Ned thought.

15

'Look out!'

Ned jerked Justus's head to the side and hit him with his spurs. The startled horse veered hard into the one ridden by John Hamlinson. As John's horse staggered, the sound of two shots, fired almost simultaneously, carried clearly in the still air.

John's reactions were nearly as swift as Ned's. Both men dived from their horses, taking cover behind brush. The horses lunged away, trotted off a short distance, then stopped, clearly confused.

At almost the same instant Ned and John caught a glimpse of motion from the edge of timber, well away from the river they were following. As if scripted by a single will, both men jerked their rifles to their shoulders and fired, in one smooth motion.

Again, as if they were following the

same hymn-book, both men jacked a new cartridge into the chamber of their rifles and sighted again, waiting for a glimpse of movement.

'You s'pect we got 'im?' the Pinkerton detective rumbled.

'I didn't hear anything that sounded like a bullet hittin' flesh.'

'Me neither.'

'There's more'n one of 'em, though.'

'Either two or three.'

'See if you can keep their heads down for a minute,' Ned said.

Even as he spoke he broke from cover and sprinted toward a stand of timber thirty yards to his left. By the time he had covered the ground he counted five shots from Hamlinson's rifle. The slugs would have likely done no damage to anything but tree branches, but they would have caused considerable disturbance in them. The sound of the rapid fire, branches breaking and flying into each other, and fragments falling all around would be enough to make the shooters duck.

In the cover of the trees Ned sprinted in an arc to try to gain a vantage point from which he could see their attackers. He had scarcely started the ploy when the sound of horses crashing through brush and timber indicated the headlong flight of the would-be bushwhackers.

Ned continued his path nonetheless, on the chance that one had stayed behind as the others fled, to try to catch them off guard. He circled around and approached the spot from which he had glimpsed the movement from deeper within the timber.

It was immediately clear that none had stayed behind. The tracks clearly indicated that three men had drawn rein at the edge of the timber, spotted him and John approaching, and decided to shoot them.

Instead of calling to Hamlinson Ned simply issued a sharp whistle. Justus instantly headed to his master, holding his head to the side to avoid stepping on the reins. As he waited for his horse Ned glanced in the direction the fleeing men had gone. Sam sat in the middle of the broken brush that marked their trail, clearly awaiting orders to follow them.

'Not now, Sam.'

The dog's ears dropped, clearly signaling his disappointment. He sat where he was, making sure Ned knew that it was not a command he agreed with.

John arrived right behind Justus. 'You coulda hollered an all-clear,' he remonstrated.

Ned shrugged. 'I called my horse. I figured even a Pinkerton guy could de-tect that they was gone from that.'

John unexpectedly grinned. 'It took me a while, but I figured it out.'

'Yeah, I was beginnin' to think I was gonna have to send my dog after you.'

'Three of 'em?'

'Yup.'

'Get a look at 'em?'

'Not even a glimpse. As soon as I made it over to the timber they jumped on their horses and hightailed it.'

'Was they followin' us?'

Ned shook his head. 'Nope. They came from the south. It looks like they just spotted us from the timber and decided to take a pot-shot at us.'

John frowned. 'Now why would they do that? Your badge ain't showin'. I don't wear one. Unless they were someone that knew one of us, why would they do that?'

Ned was struggling with the same question. 'The only thing I can think of is they're some o' the ones that've been gunnin' for me already. Whoever that is, he knows me by sight.'

'If you hadn't seen them before they shot, they would probably have gotten both of us.'

'I didn't see 'em.'

John frowned at him. 'Then why'd you ram my horse.'

'Sam told me to.'

'What?'

'Sam spotted 'em. He's got a sort of a bark that ain't really a bark when somethin' spooks 'im. As near as I can describe it, it means, 'Duck!' He don't never mean a mallard, neither. I don't never argue with it. When he makes that noise I dive for cover.'

John grinned. 'And hope the bear he barked at ain't in the bush you dive into.'

Ned shrugged his shoulders with mock seriousness. 'Well, in that case, I guess the country'd just have to make do with one less bear.'

Serious again, John said, 'Can that dog of yours follow them?'

'Yeah, he could. I ain't sure that'd be a good idea right at the present, though.'

'Why not?'

'They'll sure as anythin' lay up an' wait for us to do that. We'd be ridin' right into another ambush.'

'Could we maybe circle around them?'

'Not without knowin' where they're headin'.'

'So you just plan to let them ride off, and not even try to intercept them?'

'Yup.'

Ned mounted his horse, and nudged him southward. John followed after a long moment, nudging his horse to a lope to catch up with Justus when he'd decided Ned wasn't going to change his mind. They rode side by side for a goodly distance before either spoke.

It was Ned who broke the silence. 'You 'spect maybe them was the other three?'

John frowned. 'What other three?'

'Didn't you say there was five guys you was chasin' after?'

John's face cleared. 'There were at least five in the gang. I had only confirmed sighting of two of them heading in this direction, though.'

'Two an' three usta make five.'

'If the three that shot at us were part of the gang.'

'Any better ideas?'

'Not really.'

'Let's cut across country from here. I wanta drop in at the Rockin' R.'

'I heard a rumor circulatin' that might happen.'

The two reined away from the river and set a course directly toward the Henry ranch. Neither had any idea what awaited them there.

16

'Somethin' ain't right.'

Hamlinson looked at the sheriff, then looked back at the ranch yard. They were a good quarter-mile from it yet. They had just topped the last hill before reaching it. Ned had drawn rein when only their heads were high enough to enable them to see beyond. Or to be seen by someone there.

'Looks like a burial,' John suggested.

There was an unmistakable tone of relief in Ned's voice. 'Three wearin' dresses. That's all the women on the place, so Nellie's OK.'

As they watched, the group on the hillside above the house turned and began to walk back toward the main yard. Apparently somebody spotted them and said something. The whole group stopped instantly. Three rifles appeared, not pointed in their direction but obviously at the ready.

'I 'spect we'd best ride on in and let 'em know who we are,' Ned said.

The pair lifted their reins and rode forward. Ned was recognized in short order, and the group relaxed.

By the time they reached the yard the group had gathered in front of the main house. Everybody was curiously quiet as they approached. 'Somebody run into some hard luck?' Ned asked.

Hank's voice was hard. 'Ran into a hard chunk o' lead.'

'Who?'

'Bobby Longtree.'

'Bobby? He got shot?'

'Just about dark last night.'

'By who?'

'No idea.'

'Where?'

'Half a mile south o' the house.'

Adelia entered the conversation. 'We thought we heard a shot. Then we didn't hear anything else. Wink and Shorty were riding out this morning and found him.'

'Where'd Bobby been?'

'He'd gone to town a couple days

ago. Things was pretty slow an' he was itchin' to go to town.'

'Must've had a dust-up with someone in town, huh?'

Hank shook his head. 'No, I don't think so. If he did, whoever it was wouldn't have waited till he was pertneart back to the place here. An' Wink an' Shorty said it didn't look like there was anyone followin' 'im, or like there'd been any kind o' tussle. He didn't have no marks on 'im, like he'd been in a fight or nothin'.'

'So someone just shot 'im?'

'Sure looked that way.'

Another uneasy silence settled across the group. Then Shorty said, 'Tell him the rest, Hank.'

Hank glanced at his hired hand sharply, then looked hard at John before he looked back to Ned. He just kept looking at Ned, letting the silence ask his question.

Ned didn't notice. He was far too busy looking at Nellie. It was questionable if he even remembered where he was until Nellie said, 'I think Father wants to know who he's telling about it.'

Ned started as if he had suddenly been wakened from a sound sleep. 'Oh! Uh, yeah. Uh, sorry. I guess I'm forgettin' my manners. Folks, this here's John Hamlinson. He's a Pinkerton detective. More to that story later. John, this here's Hank an' Adelia Henry. An' that's Nellie.'

'I had that one figured out,' John said, a hint of a smile seeming irrepressible at the corners of his mouth.

As if he hadn't been interrupted Ned said, 'An' that's Wink an' Shorty an' Jim an' Lizzie. Lizzie, she's Shorty's wife. Shorty's Hank's foreman.'

'Glad to meet you all,' John responded, touching the front of his hat brim in deference to the ladies present.

'Pinkerton?' Hank demanded.

'That's right.'

'What's Pinkerton doin' up here?'

As if he were no longer part of the conversation, Ned had dismounted. He and Nellie were walking away out of everyone else's earshot, each with an arm around the other, intent on a conversation of their own. That she suddenly understood Ned had been in some considerable danger was evident from the way her hand flew up to cover her mouth. She stared at him a long moment, then flew into his arms.

The rest of the group, some smiling openly, some pretending not to notice, concentrated on their own conversation. It was suddenly up to John to fill everyone in on what had taken place.

When their curiosity had been sated, John said, 'So now, what is 'the rest' that needs to be told?'

Hank hesitated a long moment. 'Well, it seems Bobby had a watch in his pocket, and quite a bit of money when the boys found him.'

'Did he usually carry money?'

'Only when he was on the way to town, not on the way home. He never had two nickels to rub together by the time he came back from town,' the rancher said. 'And he already had a watch, and he hadn't hocked it this trip. It was still in his pocket, too.'

'Do you mind if I look at it?'

After another long hesitation the rancher fished a watch out of his trouser pocket and handed it to the detective. It was a very ornate gold watch with an equally expensive chain. John inhaled deeply.

'You recognize it?' Hank demanded.

'By description, not by sight,' John admitted.

'Where'd it come from?'

'Let me ask you a couple questions before I tell you that, if you don't mind. When did this hand of yours go to town?'

'Three days ago.'

'Just three days?'

The other hands nodded confirmation. 'That's real interesting,' John asserted. 'Real interesting.'

The others held their peace while Hamlinson visibly mulled over the information.

'Before he left and went to town, how

long had he been on the place here?'

'Over a month. That's why he was itchin' pretty bad to get to town for a while. You know how these young cowboys are. He promised to be back afore calvin' starts.'

'You're sure he didn't have a chance to be gone a few days during that time?'

'Well, yeah. I'm as sure o' that as I am that I'm standin' here.'

'Interesting.'

There was a long moment of silence. Hamlinson was obviously lost in thought, as the others stared at him in silent expectation.

At last Hank said, 'Interestin' is a plumb interestin' word. It can mean pertneart anything. So how about tellin' us what it means in this here case.'

'Oh, sorry,' Hamlinson apologized. 'I was a little lost in thought there.'

Hank's foreman couldn't resist the opening. 'I thought folks usually got lost when they was in unfamiliar territory,' Shorty offered.

John grinned in response. 'Well, now

I know why I get lost there.'

'So what're ya thinkin'? Hank demanded, refusing to share in the humor of the exchange.

'I'm thinking someone wanted your hand to get blamed for a robbery that took place just north of Denver, some three weeks ago.'

'Three weeks ago?' Adelia echoed.

'Clear down by Denver?' Wink responded.

'They ain't no way Bobby was nowheres near Denver three weeks ago,' Shorty declared. 'Every hand on the place will swear to that.'

John nodded. 'Which means either that every hand on the place is part of a roving band of outlaws, or that someone is trying to make it look like your cow-hand was involved with one.'

'You mean someone shot 'im just to try to frame 'im for a robbery?'

'Sure looks that way. Was the money he carried in gold or paper money?'

'All paper money.'

'New bills?'

'All brand-new bills. Hadn't been hardly wrinkled at all.'

Hamlinson nodded as if he had already known the answer. He looked at Hank. 'Was he riding a horse with your ranch's brand on it?'

Hank frowned and nodded. 'What would that have to do with it?'

Hamlinson thought about his answer for a long moment. Then he said, 'I'm just trying to out-guess someone I don't know. I'm trying to figure out what I might do, if I was in his shoes.'

'Whose shoes?'

'The one that's behind all the things going on.'

'Maybe you know a whole lot more about that than the rest of us do?'

'I hope so,' John shot back instantly. 'I might lose my job as a detective if I don't manage to know something everybody else doesn't already know. Are you a betting man, Mr Henry?'

Hank frowned again. 'Why?'

'I would be willing to bet you that within a day or two there will be a

United States marshal who just happens to ride in here, and he'll be asking whether anyone in your employ might happen to have some extra money and a watch that matches the description of that one.'

'Now why would he do that? I ain't seen a United States marshal in all the years I been on this place, 'cept back when they was settin' up the reservation.'

'So if one shows up now, it'll be almost certain it's because he has been tipped off by someone, and he thinks he will find evidence on your ranch of involvement in that robbery.'

Everybody stared at the detective as if he had lost his mind completely. After a moment or two Shorty said, 'You ain't makin' no sense at all.'

Hank had an entirely different take on the suggestion. 'Who is there in this here county that's got enough influence to be pullin' the strings of a US marshal?'

'Only one that I can think of.'

'Who?'

Hamlinson shook his head. 'I don't think I'm ready to go far enough to put a name on him yet. But let me make a suggestion. Put the money and the watch away, and if a marshal does show up asking about it, keep your mouths shut.'

'You mean tell 'im Bobby didn't have nothin' in his pockets?'

'Exactly.'

'I ain't in the habit o' lyin'. 'Specially to a lawman.'

'I appreciate that. But you are all certain that evidence had to have been deliberately planted on your hired hand. Let's do what we can to see that it does not accomplish what it was intended to accomplish.'

'What if no marshal shows up?'

'Then I'll have to rethink what I think is going on.'

After another long pause Hank said, 'Makes sense, I guess. At least it's worth playin' out to see what happens.'

He turned toward his hands. 'You all

heard what he said. No watch. No money. Just forget you ever saw either one.'

'Either one o' what?' Wink asked with a straight face.

'Well, git down and come in,' Hank said to Hamlinson, reverting to the standard courtesy of the range. 'I guess we sorta forgot our manners.'

'I'll take care o' your horse,' Jim offered, stepping forward. 'Ned's too.'

Hamlinson handed him the reins. 'There's an extra pair of saddle-bags on each horse. You might put them in a corner o' the barn where they ain't apt to be noticed if that marshal decides to snoop around.'

Every eye was instantly riveted on the detective. In an amazing gesture of candor and trust, he said, 'They're full of loot from that robbery, and some others.'

'The ones that froze?' Hank demanded.

Hamlinson just nodded. The others looked at each other, understanding suddenly that if the US marshal did come, and if he snooped around and found those saddlebags, everyone on the ranch would be under intense suspicion. If the marshal came with a posse, would they be in a position of having to defend themselves? Were they blithely agreeing to something that would ruin all their lives? The weight of events beyond their control suddenly settled over everyone like a pall.

17

'Looks like they're sure enough leavin' the county.'

'It does for a fact.'

Ned and John reined in beside the rutted track that followed the Wind River. A heavily loaded wagon approached, heading south. It was equipped with bows over which canvas could be spread to protect the contents, but it was open to the bright spring sunshine.

'You know 'em?'

'The Cavenaughs. They got a homestead about fifteen miles north.'

'Had a homestead, it looks like.'

The wagon was pulled by a pair of milk cows. A third cow and a pair of horses were haltered and tethered to the tailgate of the wagon. A boy of six or seven rode a third horse. A girl of three or four sat on a trunk in the center of the wagon, playing with a doll. A man and woman rode on the seat.

As they drew abreast of the two men the driver hauled on the reins. 'Whoa, up, girls,' he called to the team.

'Howdy, Ian, Mrs Cavenaugh,' Ned offered, touching the brim of his hat. 'Looks like movin' day.'

Cavenaugh looked uncomfortable. 'We figured it might be a good time to stick a plow in the ground somewhere else, Sheriff.'

'I thought you folks were doin' pretty well there on Bull Crick. That house you built there is one o' the best ones along.'

'We put a lot into it, all right. There comes a time, though, Sheriff, when a fella's gotta think of his family.'

'Why are you worried about your family?'

Cavenaugh squirmed on the wagon seat. His wife stared at him from the corner of her eyes, not turning her head. He said, 'Well, it sounds like an out an' out war's gettin' more likely every day betwixt the sheep and cattle men. Homesteaders like us'd just be plumb caught in the middle, if that happens. Then there's them Indians. Signs seem to point to them bustin' outa the reservation just about any time. There again, we'd be right plumb in the thick o' things, if that happens. We talked it over a bunch, an' decided we'd best up an' pull stakes whilst we had a good chance. Good chances don't come along all that often, you know.'

'Good chances?'

'You don't have to tell everything,' Callie Cavenaugh admonished her husband.

Ian looked at his wife and swallowed hard. He looked back at the sheriff. He looked back at his wife, visibly withering under her scowl. ''Tain't right to hold back on the sheriff,' he argued with her. 'He's got a right to know.'

Turning back to Ned before his wife could respond he said, 'The fact is, Sheriff, we got ourselves a right smart chance to sell our homestead, an' the water rights that go with it.'

'To the railroad?'

Ian frowned. He looked back and forth between John and Ned several times in obvious confusion. 'Railroad? Why would a railroad care about our homestead?'

It was Ned's turn to frown. 'Then who bought it from you?'

Ian glanced at his wife again and looked away quickly. 'That there fella that run agin' you for sheriff,' he said.

Ned and John exchanged a swift look. 'Milosevitch?' Ned demanded.

Ian nodded. 'He said he was willin' to take a chance on how things would turn out with all the trouble brewin' from all directions cuz he ain't got no family. He said if he had a family, he'd be headin' outa this country just as fast as he could go.'

'Did he pay you with paper money or gold?' John asked.

Caution drew an opaque curtain across the homesteader's eyes. 'Who're you?' he demanded.

It was Ned who responded. 'I'm sorry. I'm forgettin' my manners. Folks, this here's John Hamlinson. He's a Pinkerton detective. John, this is Ian an' Callie Cavenaugh.'

'I'm Collin,' the boy on the horse announced.

'I'm Maggie,' the girl said in a barely audible voice, staring hard at her doll instead of looking at anyone.

'You can trust John,' Ned assured the couple. 'We're working together to put a stop to the stuff that's goin' on.'

Ian hesitated a long moment, sneaking a quick glance at his wife before he answered. At last he said, 'Paper money. I'm plumb sure it's good, though. Looks good. Feels right. An' Mr Milosevitch, he wouldn't be passin' out money that wasn't no good.'

'Would you mind if I have a look at some of it?'

Ian and Callie exchanged instant looks of panic. Both looked back at the detective, then at Ned. Ned said, 'He'll give it back. It might give him some information that'll help us a lot.'

'You'll sure give it back?' Ian demanded.

'You have my word.'

'Show 'im some of it, Ma.'

'It's mostly hid here and there,' Callie resisted.

'Just show 'im what you got in your purse.'

Callie glared at her husband as if he had just betrayed a sacred trust. Her lips drew into a thin white line. When Ian refused to return her look she took a deep breath. She reached behind the seat and picked up a large handbag. Opening it she took out three twenty-dollar bills and extended them at arm's length.

John nudged his horse up beside the wagon and took the bills. He looked the crisp, new bills over quickly. He looked at Ned. He looked at the wagon, piled high with everything this family owned in the world. He took a deep breath. 'Would you mind if I trade you money?'

Suspicion deepened in Ian's look.

'Whatd'ya mean?'

John thought hard before he answered. Then he said only, 'I think this money might be important to solving the things that are going on. If you will, I'd like to trade you out of these bills. I'll give you the same amount, though.'

Ian thought it over for a long moment. A gleam flickered in his eyes briefly. 'How's about you trade me dollar for dollar, but you give me gold for the paper,' he suggested.

John thought it over. Then he said, 'Fair enough.'

He dug deeply into his pocket, dug out three double eagles and dropped them in Callie's outstretched hand. She examined the gold coins carefully, then nodded to her husband.

Ian said, 'If that'd be all you fellas are a-needin', we'll be movin' on.'

Ned gave a barely perceptible shrug. 'Well, I really think you folks are makin' a mistake, but you gotta do what you think is right.'

'At least this way we're ridin' away

with enough to start over somewhere's else.'

When neither Ned nor John responded, he picked up the reins. 'Giddup,' he called, slapping the backs of his team with the reins.

The team leaned into the harness and the procession moved on south. Ned and John sat side by side watching them until they were nearly out of sight. 'Part of the loot?'

'No question about it,' the Pinkerton man responded.

Neither man said anything for another long moment. Then it was again the Pinkerton man who spoke. 'You could've told them it was stolen money and made them give it up.'

Ned pursed his lips. 'So could you.'

'You're the sheriff.'

'Pinkerton's men is all deputy US marshals, ain't they?'

'So either one of us coulda.'

'So why didn't either one of us?'

'Because you saw the same thing in them that I did, I would guess. They were scared out of their wits. They're sure that all hell's going to break loose any day now.'

'Yeah. It looked like they had everything they own piled on that wagon. Besides, I ain't got no proof, 'cept that you think it looks like what was stolen, that it was stolen money.'

'Yeah, I got soft-hearted too,' John said, totally ignoring Ned's excuse.

'That mean neither one of us is fit to wear a badge?'

'I don't.'

'Got one in your pocket, I'm guessin', just in case you need it.'

'I don't wear it.'

'Don't make no difference.'

'No, I guess it doesn't.'

Another long silence followed as they stared at the empty road on which the wagon had long since passed from sight. Eventually John spoke. 'Well, we got what we needed, though. I guess that's a fair trade.'

'We already knew who had to be behind it all.'

'But we didn't have any proof.'

'So now we do. Now what?'

John frowned. 'How many do you figure Milo's got workin' for 'im, all told?'

'Hard to say. Anywhere from the three we know about to a dozen. Not more than a dozen. That's too many ways to split the loot and still have enough to buy out the homesteaders.'

'He won't split the loot very many ways.'

'Why not?'

'He'll kill off as many as he can when he doesn't need 'em any more.'

Ned agreed. 'That seems likely, all right. He'll keep a couple or three that he thinks he can trust. Then he'll pretend he caught the others with some o' the stolen loot, an' be a hero for bringin' 'em all to justice. Then he'll run for sheriff again.'

'Sounds like you know this fellow.'

'Better'n I'd like. If he thinks we're on to 'im, he'll be forted up plumb tight.'

'I take it you know the lie of the land at his ranch?'

'Pretty well. We'll need some help.'

'Get together a posse in town?'

Ned shook his head. 'Nah, I don't think so. We can get enough from the Rockin' R an' the Palisades.'

'I thought the Palisades was a sheep outfit?'

Ned nodded. 'It is, but they're good folks. If I can get word to Little Crow we can probably get three or four o' the reservation police to help out, too.'

John frowned. 'I don't understand what you're tryin' to do.'

Ned grinned. 'Tryin' to be just as snaky as the guy we're after. He's been doin' all this stuff to try to get three different bunches to go to war with each other. He's tryin' to get the Indians and whites to fightin' again. He's tryin' to get the sheep an' cattle men fightin' again. If all three team up together an' take out his bunch, it'll solve all the problems at once.'

'That's a pretty ambitious plan.'

'We likely oughta put it together in a hurry, too. Why don't you beat-feet it back to the Rockin' R. They know you, so they'll trust you. If that US marshal showed up like you figure, get him in on it. If he don't, make sure he don't leave the Rockin' R to go runnin' up north to let Milo know what's about to happen, though. I'll swing by the Palisades an' get Lars to head over to the Rockin' R with as many men as he can get loose from herdin' 'is sheep, then I'll swing over to the reservation an' see if I can get two or three o' them. I'll meet you back at the Rockin' R day after tomorrow.'

18

Sometimes a man just gets lucky. Ned was half way to the Palisades when Sam gave the soft warning bark, alerting Ned to approaching riders.

He reined off the trail into the edge of the trees. In minutes two horses trotted into view, coming toward him. He grinned and nudged Justus out of the trees, back on to the trail.

Lars Ingevold and Juan Rodriguez jerked their horses to a halt. Both had a hand on their guns before they recognized the sheriff.

'Now yust vat ist you hiding in dat bushes for, Sheriff?' the sheepman demanded.

'I was just headin' over to pay you a social visit.' Ned grinned.

'You vas coming ofer to eat some of my mutton,' Lars corrected.

'Well, that too.'

Lars turned to his herder. 'You haf to vatch a man vith a badge. Dey ist alvays hungry.'

'Yeah, but we always know where to get a good meal,' Ned countered.

'Alvays you know ver to get a free meal.'

Ned dropped the banter and turned serious. 'I really was headin' for your place, Lars. I don't know if you've heard, but there's a Pinkerton detective in the area.'

'I haf heard dat.'

'He's been workin' on a string o' robberies down south o' here a ways. We've got it put together, finally. The short form o' the story is this. The railroad's fixin' to put a line through along the river to open up Yellowstone Park for tourists an' such. Milosevitch figured it out, an' put together a bunch of outlaws to pull off the robberies. Now he's usin' the money from them to buy up all the land rights along the river that he can, so he can get rich off sellin' the railroad the right o' way.'

'I tell you there is something sneaky about that man,' Juan declared, staring hard at his boss.

Lars ignored him. 'You haf proofs of all dis?'

'We have proof. The Pinkerton guy identified some of the money Milo used to buy out the Cavenaughs. I ran on to a couple o' the guys in the bunch up in the mountains when we had that big snow a couple weeks ago. They had a whole bunch o' the stolen money; headin' for Milo's ranch with it.'

Lars studied the sheriff, pondering the information carefully. Then he said, 'So vat ist it dat you vill do now?'

'The Pinkerton guy is headin' back to the Rockin' R. He'll get some hands from there. Most likely ride over to the I Bar W for some, too. I was headin' over to ask you to send as many as you can spare over to the Rockin' R. Then I'm headin' over to the reservation to see if I can get two or three o' the reservation police in on it. Then we'll head up to Milo's place for a showdown.'

Once again the sheepman studied the information for a long moment. 'Do you tink you can yust get eferybody in da county to do a ting like dat together?'

'That would be a good thing, wouldn't it?'

After yet another long silence, Lars said, 'Vel, I tink so. I tink ven eferybody knows how dat man has tried to get us to all kill vun anotter, eferybody vill be mad enough vith him to stop fighting vith each other. If ve all vork together to do dis, maybe den ve can all vork together for otter things too.'

'That'd be a good thing,' Ned said again.

Lars nodded. 'Ve vill be dere. Four, I tink, ve can spare from der sheeps.'

'Four'll be just fine,' Ned agreed.

He shook hands with the sheepman and his herder, turned Justus and headed across the river, toward the ridge that marked the edge of the reservation.

'We just might manage to pull this off,' he assured either Sam or Justus. It didn't matter which one he was talking to. Neither had any intention of answering.

19

Nearly a dozen men stood scattered around the yard of the Rockin' R. There were several hands of Henry's, along with the owner, foreman and one hand from the I Bar W, Lars Ingevold, his foreman and two herders from the Palisades, John Hamlinson, the Pinkerton detective, Ned, Little Crow and Kills At Night. It was the pair from the Shoshone Reservation who were the center of a tense stand-off.

'They got no part in this.'

Ike Worley glared at the Shoshoni, who sat their horses impassively.

Ned deliberately stepped between them. He was tired. It had been a fast, hard ride to the reservation and back. It was a small miracle that he had succeeded in enlisting the broad coalition that had assembled at the Rocking R at his request.

A hard road yet lay ahead of him, before this thing was done. The last thing he wanted was to deal with a battle within this new and fragile coalition. Even so, he knew if he didn't get it adequately resolved they would have no chance to defeat Milosovitch and his men. If they did, it might well herald a period of peace and cooperation that would extend into the future, and in all likelihood save a great many lives.

He fought to keep his voice calm and reasonable. 'They got just as much business in it as the rest of us, Ike,' he argued. 'Milo's men have killed some o' their folks too.'

'Then we'll take care of it. They got no need to be here.'

'I asked 'em to join in.'

'You asked a couple savages to help us fight our fight?'

'They're reservation police. It's just as much their job as mine.'

'They got no jurisdiction off the reservation.'

'If I deputize 'em, they'll have just as much jurisdiction as you do, Ike.'

Worley's eyes fairly bugged out of his head. 'Are you tellin' me you'd deputize a couple o' them savages?'

'In a heartbeat,' Ned retorted. 'I've trusted that pair with my life more'n once.'

'Then you're a fool.'

'I'd be a bigger fool to hang on to old battle lines after a war's over with.'

Luke Tennyson, Worley's foreman, spoke up at his boss's elbow. 'I've talked with them two a couple times when we happened across 'em,' he offered. 'Once in town. Actually camped with 'em once up in the mountains. They ain't all that different from us.'

Worley whirled on his foreman as if he were going to attack him. Luke didn't back down. He met his boss's eyes calmly, and waited as if he understood, from long acquaintance, how the cattleman's mind worked.

Ned kept his voice quiet, his tone conciliatory. 'One o' Milo's men slipped over on to the reservation and shot an old woman in their village just after sunup one mornin',' he said. 'The best anybody knows, it was just to try to get 'em to come whoopin' over here somewhere to get even. Instead o' doin' that, they came to me. That's gotta say somethin' for 'em.'

Ray, Lars Ingevold's foreman spoke up. 'They shot an old woman?'

Ned nodded. 'He slipped in at night, stayed hid in the timber at sunup, waitin' for whoever came out of a tepee first. The old woman was the first one that did. He shot 'er in cold blood, then hightailed it. They followed him back to the main road along the river.'

Ray was less than convinced. 'Then how do they know it was one o' Milo's men?'

'They're trackers. They know the tracks o' that horse like you'd know the face of a man you met. They found it again later, an' seen who was ridin' it.'

'Then why didn't they do somethin' about it?'

'Because it wasn't on the reservation. They waited till they could tell me. That's what I'm tellin' you boys. We can trust 'em to ride with us.'

There was silence all around for a long moment. Then Ike said, 'Well I'll tell you one thing. I ain't lettin' 'em behind me while we're ridin'.'

He turned and stalked off. Ned turned away to hide the small smile that struggled to break loose from the corners of his mouth.

'Stop looking so smug,' a soft voice said at his elbow.

He hadn't noticed Nellie move up beside him. He swiftly made up for that lapse. He guessed it didn't matter who was looking. This was the woman he was about to marry. She didn't seem to be in the least embarrassed that he kissed her right out there in front of God and everyone. In fact, she returned it with unmistakable ardor.

'If you two can quit spoonin' long enough,' Hank interrupted, 'maybe you can tell us what we're gonna do next.'

Before Ned could say anything, John said, 'Oh, you were right about the US marshal.'

'He showed up?'

'Yup. He was here right shortly after you an' John left,' Hank confirmed. 'I been thinkin' about that. For him to show up that quick after Bobby got shot, he had to've been on the way afore it even happened. He come clear from Cheyenne.'

'He wasn't alone, either,' John put in.

'He wasn't?'

Hank jumped back into the conversation. 'The fella with him never said nothin'. I sorta had the idea he was keepin' an eye on the marshal, mostly.'

'He didn't seem too thrilled to be here, as a matter of fact,' John stated.

Ned looked back and forth between the two. 'So what did you make of it?'

John said, 'It looked to me like the marshal was pressed into coming. The other fella knew what we was supposed to've found on Bobby. The marshal asked if we found anything on him that was odd or anything. When we said 'No', that fella pertneart spit out his chew. The marshal looked plumb relieved. Hank told 'em what stuff was in Bobby's pockets, exceptin' the stuff nobody knows about, and he said, 'Well, I guess that's all I need to know'.'

'So they just left?'

The Pinkerton man looked uncomfortable. 'Well, not quite yet, then. I got a bright idea. I hope it turns out to be a good one.'

Ned's expression left no doubt he was less than pleased. 'What bright idea?'

Hamlinson took a deep breath. For the first time since he had met him, Ned thought the burly mountain of a man felt uneasy. 'Well, I got to thinking. It's not likely we could just ride up to Milosovitch's place and find him there, and his whole gang as well. They would most likely be spread out here and there, trying to scare people into quitting the county, or robbin' something else. Milosovitch himself is just as apt to be trying to buy somebody out as he is to be at his place. But if they get wind of the fact that we're about to confront him on his home ground, he'll have all his guns there and be forted up.'

Ned scowled. 'They'd be forted up, all right.'

'But they'll all be there. Anyway, I let it slip that you and I would probably find the stolen loot in a couple days, since we're pretty sure where to look.'

'And you think the marshal will go runnin' to Milo an' tell 'im?'

John shook his head. 'I think he'll hightail it right straight back to Cheyenne. It was pretty clear he wanted no part of this deal. It's the other guy that I'm betting works for Milo. Unless I miss my guess he's already there, telling Milo all about how you and me are going to come riding in like a two-man posse. Just in case we bring help, he'll call in his troops.'

Ned thought it over. 'That part of it might make sense. It means we're in for a battle, though.'

Although she remained silent, Ned felt Nellie shudder as she stood against him. He put an arm around her shoulders, offering her more of a sense of comfort and security than he felt.

20

Their timing was just about perfect. The moon was just dropping behind the Teton mountain range to the west. Heavy shadows replaced the soft white light the full moon had provided for them. Everybody was in place. It was a little over an hour before dawn.

There are two times of greatest advantage for a surprise attack. One is an hour or so after the quarry goes to sleep, when men tend to sleep the soundest. The other is just before dawn. The hour before dawn is the better of the two, especially if the prey expects an attack. The night sentries are bored sleepy by then. The daytime sentries are not yet rousted to take over. It is almost always the time of least vigilance.

They had discussed the lie of the land thoroughly en route. Ned had seen the place twice. Like most Westerners, but especially lawmen, he had the ability to recall the picture of any place he had been, and study it for details with uncanny accuracy.

The Milosovitch ranch was built to be impressive, as was everything the man did. The cut-lumber ranch house overlooked a broad, flat valley, with mountains behind it that led, in tier after tier, to the distant Absaroka Mountains. It was sided with cedar hauled all the way from Nebraska, and painted white. It boasted at least two windows of real glass in every room. A broad, roofed porch reached around the front side and both ends, making the house appear nearly twice as big as it was.

The bunkhouse was a little further along the valley, thirty yards from the house. It, too, was backed up to the timber. It had the same style of broad porch as the house, but during the time Milo had actually tried to maintain a working ranch the hands were never given enough spare time to lounge on it. Not many hands ever went back for a second stint after their first trip to town.

An equally impressive system of corrals ranged from near the bunkhouse to the big horse barn. It was one of the only barns in the county to boast paint, and its bright red coat stood out glaringly against the forest background.

Ned's ability to remember the yard's details paled in comparison to the two Shoshoni who rode with him. It was Kills At Night who mentioned the horse barn with the big haymow. Its door at the end of the barn gave a commanding view of the main approach. A man with a rifle at the edge of that door would be a very difficult target, but he could command a broad field of fire with ease.

Every man had been assigned a position and was in place with time to spare. As silently as a shadow, Kills At Night slid through a side door of the barn and up the ladder to the haymow. Hard as he tried, Ned scarcely heard the slight scuffing sound as the Shoshoni's knife eliminated the sentry so well placed in the haymow.

With equal stealth Little Crow slipped into the barn and filled a gunny sack with hay and straw. He crept to the bunkhouse. As the first light of dawn drove away the shadows of the night, he struck steel to flint and showered sparks into the hay and straw. He stepped to the bunkhouse door, opened it, threw the already smouldering bag inside and swiftly shut the door. He sprinted to the edge of the timber, where Ned tossed him his rifle.

Almost at once men began pouring out the door of the bunkhouse, coughing and swearing.

'Throw up your hands!' Ned bellowed from the trees.

He was answered by a volley of lead, fired wildly by men with smoke-filled eyes. The answering fire from the posse was much more accurate. In seconds every man in the yard was down, not moving.

The bag of smouldering hay flew out the door of the bunkhouse. A gun barrel shattered the glass of the lone window in the front. Another began to fire at anything that moved from the open door.

'Couple of 'em left inside,' Hank observed, firing in return.

'Nobody's come out've the house,' Ned worried.

As if in answer, two men burst out through the front door of the main house. One held a rifle, which he fired from the hip as fast as he could lever shells into its chamber. He had nearly emptied the magazine when he was cut down by several bullets that hit him simultaneously.

The other man emerged with a six-shooter in each hand, ducking, dodging and firing with much greater accuracy. Kills At Night, standing in the haymow door, brought him down.

'I ain't seen Milo,' Ned complained.

The words were no sooner out of his mouth that he heard a horse crashing through brush behind the house. Two shots rang out from that direction, but the noise of the fleeing horse did not stop.

Ned swore. 'He had a horse saddled an' tied out back, just in case.'

He whistled sharply. As Justus trotted out of the timber he raced to him and leaped into the saddle. 'Catch 'im, boy!' he yelled in the horse's ear as he hit him with the spurs.

The horse nearly jumped out from under him. As they darted round the corner of the house Ned spotted one of Ingevold's herders tending to somebody on the ground. In the growing light it was easy enough to see the path of broken brush and trampled grass that Milosovitch's horse had made. Justus followed it as if he read his master's mind.

Fifteen minutes later they had gained enough on their quarry to hear Milosovitch's horse ahead. Ned clung to his horse's neck, leaning as far forward as possible to keep from being raked off by the branches of the trees they raced between.

Suddenly the noise they were following ceased. Ned jerked Justus to a stop. There was no sound. 'Easy, boy,' he whispered, nudging the horse forward.

They walked slowly, as silently as possible, still following the easy trail. It opened suddenly into a grassy spot nearly twenty yards across, then closed into brush and timber again. As they started across the clearing a sharp voice cut through the silence.

'Far enough!'

Ned jerked his horse to a halt. Only then did he see Milosovitch sitting his horse at the edge of the timber, almost behind him. The man's rifle lay across his saddle, pointed directly at Ned. His hand was on the trigger. His mouth was drawn up in a tight smile.

Ned cursed himself silently, knowing he should never have given the man the opportunity to catch him flat-footed with such a rudimentary ploy.

Aloud he said, 'Give it up, Milo. There's a Pinkerton detective with us. He's got the goods on you.'

'Perhaps, but he certainly doesn't have me,' Milo answered, sounding as conversational as if he were sitting in the plush ranch house. 'I have enough in my saddlebags to be quite comfortable until I have opportunity to re-establish myself. The West is indeed a land of opportunity, Sheriff. It's too bad you won't be able to take advantage of any of those opportunities.'

In just as conversational a tone, Ned said, 'Take 'im, Sam.'

An instant of confusion crossed Milo's face, just before fifty pounds of fury barreled into him from behind. He managed to keep his seat in the saddle, but the instant of opportunity was all Ned needed. The forty-five that appeared in his hand as if of its own volition roared. Fire and lead spouted.

Milo's eyes widened. He looked down at the dog clinging to his right wrist, snarling furiously. He looked back at his adversary. He saw the smoke drifting upward from Ned's pistol. It seemed to spread and swell, until it covered his vision. He didn't understand what was happening. He didn't feel the ground as he toppled out of the saddle.

'Good dog, Sam,' was all the sheriff said.

Then, almost as if to himself, he said, 'I guess I'll be back right soon, Nellie girl.' That was suddenly what mattered most in the world.

We do hope that you have enjoyed reading this large print book.

Did you know that all of our titles are available for purchase?

We publish a wide range of high quality large print books including:
Romances, Mysteries, Classics
General Fiction
Non Fiction and Westerns

Special interest titles available in large print are:
The Little Oxford Dictionary
Music Book, Song Book
Hymn Book, Service Book

Also available from us courtesy of Oxford University Press:
Young Readers' Dictionary
(large print edition)
Young Readers' Thesaurus
(large print edition)

For further information or a free brochure, please contact us at:
Ulverscroft Large Print Books Ltd.,
The Green, Bradgate Road, Anstey,
Leicester, LE7 7FU, England.
Tel: (00 44) 0116 236 4325
Fax: (00 44) 0116 234 0205

Jeff Arlen, a detective with the Butterworth Agency, is on the trail of Alec Frome, who has stolen $10,000 from the bank where he works. Riding into Sunset Ridge, Nebraska, he hopes to find Frome in the town where he'd once lived. But, soon after his arrival, he is drawn into a perilous local battle. Capturing Frome and retrieving the stolen money looks like child's play compared to what he now faces, which will only be resolved with plenty of hot lead.

LAST STAGE FROM HELL'S MOUTH

Derek Rutherford

Sam Cotton is the last person anyone in the New Mexico town of Hope would have suspected of wrong-doing. All that changes, however, when he is seen riding away hell for leather from a scene of robbery and death. Though the victims' families save him from a lynching, once the judge arrives in town, Sam will stand trial for his life — with only his father believing in his innocence . . .

SKELETON PASS

John Russell Fearn

Prospecting for gold in the mountains, Pan Warlow discovers a bonanza — but does not live to enjoy his good fortune. Accidentally blowing himself up, he brings about a cataclysmic avalanche. Now he lies buried beneath a pile of rocks in Skeleton Pass — alongside $200,000 worth of gold belonging to wealthy banker Lanning Mackenzie. Lanning's daughter Flora is determined to find the treasure, aided by her Aunt Belinda, Dick Crespin and Black Moon. But she is in danger from the notorious outlaw Loupe Vanquera . . .

DEAD MAN'S CANYON

Terrell L. Bowers

After the Civil War, former ranger Nicolas Kilpatrick and his fellow ex-soldiers continue to deploy their skills, protecting settlers from Indian attacks and tracking down gangs of robbers and rustlers. In the wake of a shootout with the murderous Maitland Guerrillas, a dying bandit offers Nick information on the gang's leader — in exchange for a promise that his soon-to-be-widow will be taken care of. Setting off to chase down Frank Maitland and keep his vow, Nick heads out to Laramie . . .

LONGHORN JUSTICE

Will DuRey

Cattle baron Nat Erdlatter has built his empire by taking what he wants, then ruthlessly holding on to it. Even now, with the Homestead Act encouraging people to claim their own portions of land, he believes that his needs take precedence over the government's decrees. But times are changing, and the citizens of nearby Enterprise are angered by his latest callous act — none more so than his ranch hands Clem Rawlings and Gus Farley, who become embroiled in an affair that can only lead to violence and danger . . .